ABOUT THE AUTHOR

Brian Jarman was born on a farm in Mid-Wales, the joint youngest of five brothers. After studying in London, Paris and Cardiff, he joined the South Wales Argus as a reporter and then worked for the BBC for 22 years, mainly as a current affairs editor at The World Service. He's now Senior Lecturer in Journalism at London Metropolitan University. He's published two other novels, *The Missing Room* and *The Fall From Howling Hill*

Published by Fitzrovia Books, London
Copyright © 2017 by Brian Jarman
Front cover photograph © 2017 Charles Newbold
All rights reserved
ISBN-13: 978-1975620127
ISBN-10: 1975620127

REVIEWS FOR *THE MISSING ROOM*

I loved it. Its a fine novel, very well plotted, full of character, and I couldn't put it down.
Carmen Callil, founder of Virago Press

An ingenious page turner, but with the power to encourage reflection on the human condition - it's all there: family, health, career, and of course the slippery slope to alcoholism.
Clive Jennings, Director of the National Print Gallery

Simply on the strength of a piece of fiction about ME from a male point of view, Jarman deserves 5 stars. And, there is a lot more. The writing is strong - Mr. Jarman is not only a fine journalist but a great storyteller.
Pamela Post-Ferrante, writer and lecturer

In memory of
Lilian Nagler
and of Brynnar and Maisie Jones, with fond memories of visits to the Rhondda

Dedicated to two great storytellers, Bob Ferrante and Pamela Post-Ferrante, with thanks for their friendship and support

The author also gives heartfelt thanks to his editors Annabel Hughes and Ella Jones-Keller, to cousin Meryl Lewis for her memories of growing up in the Rhondda, to Charles Newbold for the cover photo, and to Caroline Collyer for her assurance that she loved the story despite her scant interest in Bridge

The moment a hand of bridge is dealt, the two partnerships begin to jostle for position. During both bidding and play, when one side takes action, the other endeavours to counter it - and the action taken cannot be random: it must be a direct response to the aims and strategies of the opposing side.

BRIDGE: WINNING WAYS TO PLAY YOUR CARDS   Paul Mendelson

If you've made it this far, Bravo!
Nina's pen is useless

Oct 2021

The Final Trick

by Brian Jarman

Chapter One

Not long after I first encountered Greta, I began to think of her as the rudest woman in the world, or at least the rudest I'd ever met. Shortly after that, I became determined to find one redeeming feature about her, her One Good Thing. Many times I made up my mind never to see her again, but by then she had her somewhat bizarre hold on me.

I was in a dark place then, still convinced that I'd never get over getting over Megan. Nor did I want to. I certainly could not have predicted the form my salvation would take. How I crossed Greta's path in the first place, in a Bridge club in Manhattan in the late 90s, is bit of a story. It began thousands of miles away in Wales, one spring evening. What happened there made me wonder if people come into your life for a reason, and indeed if people leave it for a reason too

Dumped after ten years' marriage, fairly happy years, I'd thought, without really thinking about it at all. Of course we'd had the inevitable ups and downs - who doesn't in ten years? But I believed we'd weathered them, come out stronger even, understood each other, were friends. I cannot bear to picture it even now, that night, but it comes back to me all of a sudden sometimes. She sat there so coolly, sipping a large Pinot Grigio and smoking one of those long brown cigarettes of hers.

We were in a new-fangled bistro, on an upstairs outside terrace overlooking Cardiff Bay. Tiger Bay, it was in my younger days, with its dreary aspect over the depressing, ugly mudflats stretching out into the Bristol Channel. Yet it had a certain witty, gritty personality and distinctive face, the fire escapes on the weathered mercantile buildings lending it an American air. Now it was all marina, restaurants, sophistication, blah.

'I need my space', said Megan (never Meg), blowing smoke forcefully above my head, not looking me in the eye for more than a second or two at a time.

'What does that mean - a kitchen extension?' At the best of times, I knew I sneered at what I regarded as psychobabble, and at the worst of times, such as then, I could lapse into sarcasm. Always Megan ignored it.

'It's just that whatever you do is more important than what I do,' she said, so coolly, her determination steely.

'That's unfair.' It came out as a shout. I lowered my voice. 'I have the greatest respect - admiration - for your job. Far more interesting than mine.'

'It's the little things in life,' she continued, as if from a prepared speech. 'Going back to the kitchen, whenever you're cooking that takes precedence. You just think I'm in the way if I'm there trying to do something.'

'Well sometimes you are……..' Megan's glare suggested I should change tack.

'It's just that I have to concentrate - I'm in my groove, have my routine.'

'That's just what I mean. Don't I? You're a kitchen dictator. And then there's holidays.'

'What about them?' We both loved travelling.

'We always do what you want to do.'

'You're always happy to leave it to me.'

'Not happy. You present me with a plan. It's easier.'

'But you don't come up with plans yourself.....'

I could suddenly hear that I was conforming to the stereotype of the controlling husband that she was presenting.

I went on the attack with the one question I really wanted to ask.

She gave an exasperated sigh.

'No, there's no one else. Oh, don't try to change my mind, Al,' (never Alun) she said when I sat there in silence. 'It's pointless. It's over. I just can't go on like this. I want to live my own life now.'

'Don't you love me anymore?' I stifled a sob.

She stubbed her cigarette out aggressively in the tin ashtray. It rattled. She smoked those long thin brown ones which were all the rage back then.

'I'll always love you, Al. I just can't live with you. That's why we need a clean break.'

'I can change,' I said feebly, conscious that this was the standard script. 'You've made me think. It's hard to see yourself the way others do. I thought we were OK, but now you've given me some pointers I can mend my ways. Let's at least give it a whirl. Try it for a few months.'

'No,' she said, still stabbing her dead cigarette butt. 'I've said these things before. Many times. You weren't listening. You never listen.'

Another silence between us. Downstairs there was a private party. Michael Jackson's *You Are Not* Alone was blaring away, competing with the sound of merry revellers.

'What more do you want me to say?' she said at last.

I didn't want her to say anything more. I wished she hadn't said as much. In that first, unspeakable shock the only thought I had was that I was going to keel over, slip from my chair onto the floor like something from an awful comedy sketch. I felt light-headed, terrified of the yawning chasm of pointlessness that in an instant had become my life. When I first met her I loved the fact that she was uncompromising. All or nothing. She was still my all. And now I was her nothing, whatever fine words she uttered.

That was the time, when we met, that we still believed that we were equals, didn't question the concept at all, what it would mean in practice, in life. I remembered an old great uncle of mine telling me once, when I just started courting as he would have put it, that up to the age of thirty women believe they're unique. Then the humdrum overwhelms them. Life hits them in the face just when they thought they'd made a friend of it. Then they blame you and never forgive you. I thought he was a sexist old git. But maybe there was something in it.

'This isn't easy for me either, you know,' said Always Megan, now looking at the boats bobbing on the cold darkening water down below.

There was nothing I could say to that. There was nothing I could say to anything. She was right, in a way. It was pointless to linger. If she said it was over, then it must be. I wanted to ask her exactly what the 'like this' was that she couldn't go on with. But something stopped me. It was my fault, perhaps, that I hadn't seen it coming. That in itself was a bad sign of something.

It couldn't have come at a worse time for me, although when is a good time for such announcements? My job at the university, lecturing in Journalism, seemed to be going nowhere. For some time I'd been thinking I should be doing something else, but not doing anything about it. Her career as a producer at the BBC, on the other hand, was flourishing, and she loved it, loved the people, the buzz, the glamour, I suppose.

I couldn't quite believe there was no-one else, although why would she lie at a moment like this? Maybe she meant there was no-<u>one</u> else. Maybe there were several elses. Maybe I'd become boring, rutted - and obviously dispensable.

And yet I grasped for something I could say that would make her change her mind and stay, even though deep down a terrible tremor told me that nothing could. There was so much I wanted to say, felt I should say, and yet I was speechless. And anyway my mouth was so dry it felt as if my tongue was glued to the roof.

At that moment I hated her in a way I've never hated anyone, while not stopping loving her for a second. I never had done, from the first moment our eyes locked across that crowded pub in Roath. But a vivid image came into my mind's eye. It was me holding a shiny gun to that shiny black hair of hers, squeezing a trigger and putting a bullet into that treacherous head. If I had a gun to hand I would have. The thought alarmed me, and brought me back to my senses, what were left of them.

When I managed to focus again on what she was saying, she was offering to move out of the house, and go to stay with Eleri. It was as if she was making plans for Christmas instead of ending our life together. Eleri. Never liked her. She was of the 'all men are bastards' school. You only had to look at her for her to inject some sinister meaning into it. So I tried to avoid meeting her if at all possible. I told Megan she could stay in our house. I'd find somewhere to go. I didn't care if I never saw the place again. I wanted to get away.

Why wasn't I putting up a fight? She didn't seem surprised or bothered that much when I told her that I'd go and see if I could stay with Nick. He had a flat in one of those big houses on Cathedral Road. I left her in the restaurant, staggered back to our house, and packed a bag there and then.

That night, in the rusting single bed in his spare room, I tossed and turned, trying to work out how to go on. This was never meant to happen to me; it happened to others. And how lightly we all treated their tales of woe when it did. We'd blithely count off on our fingers their reasons to be cheerful, grateful even. Yet even though we can always seem to find something positive in the lives of others, I could find not a single one in my own. All sense of purpose and direction had vanished from my life, and I didn't even have enough oomph to want it back.

Over the next few days I fell into some kind of automated routine, picking up things from the house when I knew Megan would be at work, turning up for classes looking no doubt a total write-off, doing the minimum and hoping to get away with it. To Nick I simply said Megan and I were having problems, and he's the kind of guy who lets you be, who would check to see if you wanted to talk and if you didn't would wait until you did. I'd chosen my helpmate well. We went for a few pints in the evening to the Halfway. Nick was skilled at keeping up a good level of conversation - films, music, politics, sport - and ignoring the fact that I didn't have much to say.

In that time-honoured phrase, I went through the motions, but even that took an almost superhuman effort. I would have to prompt myself to do the most basic things. Get out of bed. Stagger to the bathroom. Go to the toilet. Brush teeth. Deodorise. Find clean pants. Put them on. Find clean shirt, or a dirty one would do. Put it on. Find clean socks. You get the idea. In the morning I was all but overwhelmed by the prospect of getting through another day, and in the evening, another night.

The initial shock morphed into fury. I was furious that she could so casually end it all. I would have been hard pressed to say though what would have been a better way - weeping and wailing with an operatic aria?

It shook me out of my torpor and called me to action. It wasn't a good action.

I couldn't stop dwelling on the suspected Someone Else. I borrowed a car from my friend Les, a photographer on the Welsh Mail I knew from the time I worked there. He used to work on the nationals in London and sometimes had to do overnight doorsteps. His Polo had those stick-on shades on the back windows which provided cover. He told me to take a sleeping bag in case I had to spend the night, sandwiches and a flask of tea, and a bottle to pee in. He also told me not to be so stupid.

One Friday evening I drove down to the Esplanade and parked a few houses down from ours, but where I had a good view of our front door. Ours? Hers. It was before she would be home from work. I settled down in the back seat with *Bleak House* to while away the time, but couldn't concentrate. She didn't come back at the usual time - she must have gone out. Fortunately it was a quiet street so it was noticeable when someone drove up or walked by. I had to wait until eleven before I heard footsteps tottering along the pavement behind the car. There were two pairs: the click of high heels and the soft plod of trainers. There was giggling. I wriggled into position where I could peer out of the small gap between the shade and the window rim. As the heels and trainers and giggles came alongside the car, my heart thumped so hard it almost drowned them out. The ridiculousness of the situation hit me. Surely they would rumble me.

The steps passed by, and my heart quietened down a little. The pair stopped outside her front door as she looked clumsily in her bag for keys. I lifted Les' binoculars and got a good view of Someone Else by the light of the street lamp. Late twenties, I would say, with a trendy clipped beard and short blond hair. Never seen him before in my life. She looked happier than I'd seen her in ages, a look I'd almost forgotten. She found her keys and in they went.

I waited until midnight then set my travel alarm clock for 6.30. Needn't have bothered, of course, as I merely dozed fitfully and was fully awake by six. Had a pee in the bottle, munched a bit of BLT, and took some wonderful slurps of hot tea. Bless Les.

It wasn't until eight that the front door opened. Out stepped Someone Else, looking ruffled but rather pleased with himself. No wave back as he closed the door. She usually left at 8.45, so maybe was still in bed. There it was then. I'd been right all along. Numbly I drove up through Grangetown to avoid the rush in the centre, and round to Cathedral Road. Nick would have left by now. I fell onto my bed, figuring I'd ponder my next move, but unexpectedly went to sleep straight way and dreamed I was in a shop that sold plastic toy weapons in gaudy colours. And in my head five words looped around and around.

It can't end like this.

Chapter Two

I woke with a jolt and checked my watch. It was gone twelve, and I jumped out of bed in a panic. I'd missed a class. Then I remembered it was Saturday, and sat on the bed waiting for my heartbeat to subside to sustainable levels. Saturdays had always been black for me. I'm one of those people who see days of the week in colour. A few people do but most don't. Synaesthesia, I believe it's called. Mondays are deep blue, Tuesdays primrose yellow, Wednesdays red, Thursdays grey with a little rush icon in the middle, Fridays off-white, Saturdays black, and Sundays like sandpaper. It's something you can't help. I remember a colleague of Megan's interviewing me for some programme she was making. She had it too, but her colours were all wrong (how could Mondays possibly be pink?). At the end of the interview she laughed and said, 'Al - you're mad.'

So here we were, on black Saturday. There was something I had to do. I couldn't figure out what, although had a vague sense of it, like a dream instantly forgotten. The dream……..the toy gun shop. That was it. Someone Else. I had to find out who Someone Else was.

I drove Les' car to his place up in Llandaff, formulating a plan on the way. He could only have met Megan a couple of brief times, but had one or two friends at the Beeb. If he went to the Conway, he could put some feelers out about what she was up to. It was one of the main watering holes of the BBC crowd in Pontcanna, known as the Media Triangle with its large stone bay-fronted houses and grassy verges.

He was pleased at getting his car back so promptly, but hesitant about agreeing to my latest request.

'Look, I know it's a bit of an imposition, but couldn't you just go to the Conway for a few drinks and ask a few discreet questions? I could meet you in the Romilly afterwards for a debriefing. The Romilly's off the Beeb's beat. I'll stand you the drinks.'

'It's not that, Al. It's just that I'm not sure I should be going along with this scheme of yours. What good can come of it?'

'Don't you think it's good for me to be doing something rather than moping around wallowing in my misery?'

'Look, of course I do sympathise, but don't you think you'd be better off trying to put it behind you and move on?'

'That's what I'm trying to do, and maybe this will help me.'

'Well, what do you plan on doing if we do find out who this Someone Else is?'

'I don't have a plan, Les. But I do have to know.'

'I might not find out anything at all.'

'It's worth a shot, Les. Just this once.'

'Ok, as long as you make me a solemn promise.'

'What?'

'Just don't do anything silly.'

'Scout's honour,' I said, holding my hand up in the recognised manner.

I got to the Romilly about nine. No sign of Les, or indeed anyone else I knew. The place was unloved and unfrequented, and it was a grim hour or two sitting at the bar nursing a couple of pints, watching the door and willing it to open.

At just after ten it did, and in walked Les, looking quite pleased with himself, if it wasn't just wishful thinking on my part. We got more drinks and went to sit in the corner of the near-empty bar.

He said there were a few from the Beeb at the Conway, including a director who worked on *Focus Wales*, Megan's current affairs programme.

'They've got a new researcher,' said Les. 'Mark. He's lodging with Megan pro tem.'

'Lodging?' I challenged, as if cross-examining someone in a witness box.

'And he's gay.'

'Gay?'

'Yes. Why are you repeating everything?'

'I'm just trying to take it in. Are you sure?'

'Yes, I didn't even have to ask many questions. They were all talking about it. And for the record, they're convinced that there is no Someone Else.

There was relief of course, but also frustration that I'd come up a blind alley, with nowhere else to go. And after this short-lived spurt of action, I fell back into a rather comatose state, hunkering down in Nick's spare room. As hard as I tried, I couldn't stop replaying her words back in my head which implied I was selfish and even controlling. I couldn't fit this in with my own image of myself. Was that part of the problem - that I was unaware of my own shortcomings?

I had a soundtrack to my misery. Over and over I played Jacques Brel, that master of the mournful who could make the most wretched mood romantic, heroic even. I'd got to know him when I lived in Brussels for a year after university. Not personally, you understand. I'd always felt there was an affinity between Wales and Belgium: small, bilingual, overshadowed by a larger, more glamorous neighbour, the butt of their jokes. I'd have to concede there was not all that much commonality in *Le Plat Pays Qui Est Le Mien*. But on and on it went, with headphones and a couple of brandies after Nick had gone to bed. It had the line '*avec le fil de jours pour unique voyage*' ('with the passing of days as my only travel'), which was more like it. Even more ironic was *Quand On A Que L'amour* (When You Only Have Love) which lists all the things you don't have but ends on the triumphant note that if you have only love and nothing else, you're king of the whole world. And of course love was the one thing I no longer had. More appropriate was the song *J'arrive* - I'm coming - which is what a dying man shouts to the heavens while listing all the things he wished he'd done. *Deux chrysanthemes*, he kept singing, *deux chrysantemes*. Chrysanthemums being the French flower of death. Oh yes, I almost enjoyed my misery then.

I began to fear that I was losing it – losing it my grip on reality. At times it seemed quite literally to recede before my eyes: the room would drift away from me like a visual effect in a sci-fi film. This happened more than once when I was lecturing to my students and for the first time in years I began to get nervous before a lecture, like when I first started. I sought out an old friend of mine, Mari, a psychotherapist.

'Thank God your stalking did take you up a blind alley,' she said over coffee in a little caff in one of the arcades. 'Who knows where it would have led? At least you had the wherewithal to realise you were behaving a little irrationally and to lay off.'

Her eyes swept over me from head to foot.

'You're not looking so good,' she said 'Try to focus on the basics of life. And get out more. Get an interest. Doesn't have to be major. Think what gets you out of yourself . One of the first signs of mental illness is lack of personal hygiene. Try to look after yourself. Don't let yourself go.'

Easy for her to say. Most of the time I wanted to let myself go, couldn't see the point in doing otherwise. But I managed to hang on. Just.

So far I hadn't been able to face telling my family. But Cardiff is a small place and Taff's Well, the village where my parents lived in the valley to the north, even smaller. Word was bound to get around before long. Two or three weeks after it happened, my sister Kath rang my mobile.

'What's up?' she asked in her no-nonsense way. I couldn't tell whether this was a general enquiry or she'd already heard something.

'Me and Megan have been having some problems,' I said, 'and I'm staying with Nick for a few days.'

'Want to talk about it?'

'Not really.'

'Well, you'll have to sooner or later,' said Kath. 'Let's meet up for a drink.'

Kath was kept busy with her two young kids and a part time job at the library. This was a generous offer, one I could hardly refuse.

So a couple of days later we found ourselves in the Old Arcade, the sprawling, scruffy, boisterous pub in the centre of town that was one of the hubs on international day, when Wales played at home at the Arms Park. The walls were covered with framed rugby shirts of clubs and nations. It was a good choice for such a meeting, with just the right degree of anonymity and background chatter to make talking easy. I was soon baring my soul to Kath.

'Megan's dumped me,' I said. 'It's over,' coming right out with it in a way I hadn't fully admitted to myself before.

Kate was unfazed, down to earth. She asked a few questions, which rammed it home further to me what a pickle I was in.

'You're going to have to tell Mam and Dad before they find out from someone else. They'll be hurt if they do,' said Kath.

I knew this to be true. They were fond of Megan.

'Had you heard anything yourself?'

'Mike heard a rumour.'

Of course. Mike worked at HTV. They moved in the same circles.

'I'll go up and see them soon,' I promised.

'Don't leave it too long,' she said. 'I know you. Meanwhile, what are you doing with yourself?'

'Not much.'

'You shouldn't sit around and mope. That won't get you anywhere. You need to get out and do something.'

'What?'

'Why don't you come and play Bridge with me at the club. You used to like it.'

Bridge. What a strange suggestion at a time like this, I thought. I probably wouldn't be able to concentrate on the cards. She was right though, I did used to like it. We'd played a lot of cards when we were younger, especially around Christmas. Mam is from rural Mid-Wales and there I gather whist drives were one of the main sources of entertainment on cold and dark winter nights. At home the four of us would play – Mam and Kath against me and Dad. At school a bunch of us used to play poker at dinnertime, until a boy called Robert Harley came from England and started teaching us Bridge. Thinking back, it was strange that he remained Robert, managing to avoid the Welsh habit of reducing names to one syllable. No Bob or Rob he. He was something of a maths whizz-kid and I believe went on to write a bridge column in a national newspaper.

At first the rest of us were not that keen: the game required too much concentration and seemed more like maths homework than fun. But he persevered, insisting that Bridge is a superior game because it's more about skill than chance. It's played like whist but has the extra dimension that pairs of players must bid for trumps, whereas in whist trumps are determined by a simple rotation of the suits.

In time Robert and a couple of friends started coming round to our place to play. Soon Kath got roped in too, when we needed a fourth. She became a good player. We joined a Bridge club in Pontcanna. I did enjoy it for a while but forgot about it when I went to university in Bristol. Too many other things to do. It was Kath who kept it up, and still liked playing whenever she could.

I didn't feel up to it, and tried to be non-committal, but Kath was having none of it.

'We'll go on Thursday,' she said. 'I'll call for you at Nick's.'

Nick was out when I got back, so I took a deep breath and rang Mam. I told her Megan and I had been having some problems, and I was staying with a friend. I could tell she was upset, but put a brave face, or rather voice on it for my sake, I supposed.

'Is there any hope for you two?' she asked in the small, mournful voice she used for family tragedies.

'Well, there's always hope,' I said cheerfully, feeling no cheer whatsoever.

Chapter Three

I rang Kath the evening before we were due to play Bridge to call it off. I couldn't face people. I'd forgotten how to play, I told her.

'Rubbish,' she said. 'All you need to do is remember to count your points, and the rest will fall into place. You do remember how to count your points, don't you?'

'Of course I do. Four for an ace, three for a king, two for a queen, and one for a jack.'

'And how many points do you need to be able to bid?'

'Twelve.'

Before I knew it, I was complicit in her scheme. Well played, Kath.

'There you are. Perfect. I'll be round at seven.'

I was dreading it.

The club was exactly like I remembered it. It had been more than ten years since I'd been there. It was held upstairs in a pub called The Blue Angel, something of a gathering place for Welsh speakers. The room was kept for special occasions and private parties, I suppose. It had a depressing, unused, musty atmosphere, with dark mock Jacobean furniture and a barely-stocked bar.

As we walked in, an elderly couple I thought I recognised were putting green baize cloths on the tables, and unpacking the red bidding boxes and card trays from cardboard boxes balanced on a couple of chairs in the corner. They said hello to Kath and gave me a brief nod when she introduced me, concentrating on their task.

There's a lot more to remember when you play in a club - the process itself and the strict etiquette you have to observe. Nothing is quite like when you play at home. It's very daunting.

Duplicate Bridge means everyone in the club (in Pontcanna there were usually about ten tables) gets to play the same hands, so each pair competes with all the others for the most points. The hands are dealt out beforehand and put in special metal trays, divided into North, West etc. The trays are placed in the middle of the table, four at a time, with a little arrow pointing to the dealer so you know who should start the bidding. As you play, the cards are not piled on top of each other in the middle of the table, but placed down in front of you. If you win the trick you place your card face-down in front of you, short side facing you. If you lose, you place it lengthwise, pointing at your opponents. After the hand is over you gather up your cards and put them in your designated section of the metal tray. Once the four hands have been played, the four boxes are passed anti-clockwise around the room to the next table and a new set of boxes are passed to your table. North and South stay where they are, and East and West move one table clockwise. So by the end of the evening, all partnerships will have played all the East/West or North/South hands. Simple, huh?

There's more. Because you're competing with everyone else, you don't speak your bids. Instead you have a bidding box, holding cards emblazoned with every possible bid: 1D, 2S, 3NT (No Trumps), PASS, etc. The boxes are almost invariably red plastic, and kept on your right hand side (if you're right-handed) on the table. They can be very fiddly, especially in the beginning for fumbling and slightly shaking fingers like mine were. And then if you make a mistake there's the lurking figure of the Director whom your opponents can call over. He has a number of punishments at his disposal if he finds you've erred - he can fine you tricks for example or declare the game void.

Kath suggested we sit in the East/West position, so we could avoid scoring, which is North's job. Kath had never completely mastered the scoring and I sure as hell hadn't. We were playing against two scruffy middle-aged guys who seemed to know what they were doing. As I picked up my hand, my own hands were shaking quite visibly. When I tried to steady them, the shaking became worse.

My cards were:

S   K J 7
H   A K 10 9
D   Q J 4
C   J 5 3

I had fifteen points. I looked at Kath. She was concentrating on sorting her cards out in her hand, her face inscrutable. As I was the dealer, I had to start or 'open' the bidding. This was quite a straightforward bid, thank God. You have to have at least four cards in any suit to bid it, so I opened one heart. That's saying in effect, 'If hearts were trumps, we can make a majority of tricks. What do you think, partner?' There are thirteen tricks to be made in each hand. If you bid one of a suit, you're saying you'll make at least the smallest majority (or one more than the minority of six).

My left hand opponent passed. It was now up to Kath to 'reply' to my bid. She would pass if she had less than six points. If she had six or more she could make her own bid, raising my hearts if she had at least four of them or naming her own suit if she didn't. Bridge is all about the partnership, communicating by the bidding what you have in your hand. Kath pondered for a moment or two then bid three hearts. That was a jump bid, bypassing the more usual bid of two hearts, and meant she had between ten and twelve points and at least four hearts. Together we had eight hearts (meaning the opponents would have only five between them) and between 25 and 27 points out of a total of 40. You need 26 points to make a game in four hearts, so that's what I bid when it was my turn again. The opponents hadn't bid at all.

We made it exactly. It was a routine contract, and straightforward to play, so I shouldn't have felt as pleased with myself as I did. Kath gave me a huge smile of encouragement, and my hands stopped shaking. I began to get into the game, forgetting my troubles for the first time in days.

Kath and I came sixth or seventh overall, which wasn't too bad in the circumstances. It took me out of myself, as Mari had suggested and gave me a lift, a tiny ray of hope that there may be life after Megan. But in the following days I sank down again, as realities had to be faced. There were things I needed to pick up from the house, and indeed questions about the future of the house and mortgage. For these reasons I gave myself permission to ring Megan, something I'd been itching to do for a while now but had managed to control myself. As I dialled the numbers which had now taken on an almost mystical quality, my mouth was so dry it almost stuck shut and I wondered if I'd be able to speak. I needn't have worried. As I should have predicted, I got her voicemail. And the next day. And the next.

Kath came to my rescue once again. She phoned Megan and arranged for the two of us to go around to the house while Megan was out to pack up bags of clothes and books. Kath had asked her about financial arrangements, but she didn't seem to want to discuss them. Well, on her own head be it. I'd continue to make the mortgage payments and the house was still half mine. I was relieved that there was no talk of divorce, for the moment at least. There were no kids, and the car was hers.

I began to feel that I would have to get away, way away, as the only way out. I thought of it as rebooting my life, starting from scratch, experiencing everything anew. I dredged from somewhere in my addled memory a half-baked plan for a year's exchange with a media lecturer in New York. Tyler Gates was his unlikely name. I rang to check if he was still interested. He'd instigated the idea in the first place a couple of years ago but it had got nowhere - mainly due to my dithering, I now saw. And that was mainly due, irony of ironies, to Megan's concerns about spending a year apart.

'Sure thing,' said Tyler.

'Could you make it the start of this next academic year?'

'Sure can.'

I went to see the Dean, but he wasn't keen. I'd left it too late, and it would take too much organisation.

'Tyler's on for it and I'll handle everything, briefing him, timetables etc,' I said. We'd already done a lot of the groundwork, checking that our journalism courses were compatible, swapping lecture plans, ensuring that we could adapt our material to each other's media industry and even bring an extra dimension from experience of working in a different country. At the time, Cardiff had one of the best reputations in Britain for its journalism school, known locally as The College of Knowledge. It was one of the first, and a good match for Stuyvesant's.

I could tell I still didn't have the Dean's full engagement.

'Look, I really need this time away. For personal reasons as much as anything else.' Always a hard one to argue with.

'Very well', he sighed. 'Take care of it.'

It was one of those things that came together remarkably easily once I'd made my mind up. The faculties agreed to it, as long as we wrote a joint paper together at the end of it. Tyler's university in New York – Stuyvesant - got some grant from somewhere and wanted the focus to be public broadcasting in the two countries. Tyler and I jumped at it. They agreed to put us up in a reasonably-priced hotel for a month while we found somewhere to stay, and then give a small allowance towards rent.

Tyler, like so many of his compatriots, was good at recommendations and touted an old hotel in Greenwich Village, The Wayside Inn. He described it as 'three old townhouses knocked into one, with many original features and an eclectic, not to say eccentric collection of antiquities, and not as costly as you might think'. OK by me.

It wasn't easy for me to come up with a satisfying reciprocal suggestion, but I settled on what I still thought of as The Big Windsor, a big (oddly enough) hotel on the seafront we used to go to as students in what was still Tiger Bay. I was doing a post-graduate diploma in journalism at the College of Knowledge. Eight of us lived nearby in a slummy old Captain's house on the Esplanade near our house, Megan's and mine. It was a rat hole, literally.   The student house, I mean. So was the pub, come to think of it. The rats ran across the kitchen floor from the rubbish dump out back, trying to take refuge, it seemed, in the mould-accented bathroom that opened, illegally, off it.

The Big Windsor then was little more than a tarts' and tars' pub. If any male in our group so much as said hi to one of the local girls, she'd ask what ship he was from and eye up the women with us with a warning glint. It was a throwback to the time when Tiger Bay really was a crossroads of the Seven Seas, if I'm not mixing metaphors too wantonly. It was a melting pot long before the phrase was coined. Alongside The Big Windsor, grand old dilapidated bank buildings memorialised the onetime commerce of the bay area, when all the coal from the valleys that fan around Cardiff was shipped out God knows where. With the iron fire-escapes running down their facades to piles of rubble below where back-to-backs had been pulled down, they gave a hint of old inner American cities. Maybe that's why I thought of Tyler. And by living there in the student house we thought we were getting right down to the witty, gritty soul of old Tiger Bay.

Now the place was transformed, for better or worse was hard to say. Boardwalks, hotels, restaurants and exhibition spaces had replaced the rubble, and later would come the gigantic crag of the Millennium Centre and the flimsy glass of the National Assembly.

I went down one evening with Nick to check out The Big Windsor, now the Cardiff Bay Hotel. Outside it still had its old look of a rather grand Victorian railway station, but not a square inch of the interior was recognisable from the old days. It was all chrome and uplighting. Not a tar or tart in sight. I wondered vaguely where they went these days. I tried to hear again the voices of husky Beryl the landlady - Beryl the Peril - and Gappy George the barman, so called because of the huge gap in his front teeth. After we'd all got to like him, he was put inside for rape, although he was adamant there was consent. Beryl had asked me to go with her to see him in Cardiff Jail. I was uneasy about it on so many levels but was too cowardly to say so. It was the first time I'd been inside a prison, and I hoped to God it would be the last. I was chewing gum and Gappy George stretched out his hand for one. A guard appeared instantly and forbade it.

I could no longer hear those voices in the old Big Windsor. More goodbyes. But by now I was getting ready to say them.

So I suggested The Big Windsor to Tyler.

'Just the ticket,' he wrote back. I didn't think Americans said just the ticket. Maybe he was trying to sound English.

A couple of weeks before I was due to fly to JFK, Kath urged me to go for one more night at the Bridge Club. What did I have to lose? But when I got there, I couldn't see her. A smallish woman with fly-blown hair came up to me and said, 'You must be Al.'

'Yes, I must,' said I.

'Hi, I'm Mary,' she said, holding out her hand in a forthright manner and giving mine a hearty shake. It was only later that I discovered she was known in the club as Scary Mary. 'Kath's sorry, but she can't make it. I'll play with you instead.'

The scheming little so-and-so, I thought, although perhaps it was another word that crept into my mind. I had no choice. I was cornered.

It was something of a disastrous pairing. Scary Mary was a tournament player who'd been Welsh regional champion or something. She was a barrister with the Crown Prosecution Service, and I felt in the dock myself when she berated me after almost every game for not bidding or playing correctly.

On one hand she opened 1C, and as I had 12 points I jumped to 2NT.

'I don't know what that means,' mumbled Scary Mary with a sigh.

This was against protocol - players are not supposed to talk during the bidding.

'Neither do I,' I said under my breath and we ended up in the wrong contract which we didn't make. Scary Mary set to, saying I should have bid this, that and the other. One of our opponents left the table and came back with the Director, a matronly woman.

'Are you arguing?' she said, looking directly at me.

'I'm listening,' I said, sweeping my gaze over to Scary Mary.

The Director addressed her.

'We like to keep things polite here,' she said. 'Have you got anything to say to him?' She nodded at the opponent who had taken his seat again and clearly meant an apology was called for.

Scary Mary looked him square in the eye.

'Yes. Fuck off.'

The Director took a step back in alarm.

'Now look, we're a friendly club. We don't want any of that language here.'

'Well, can I hit him then?'

The Director backed off, not knowing how to handle the situation. The opponent was looking down at the table. Scary Mary carried on as if nothing had happened.

'What on earth were you thinking?' I said when I next saw Kath.

'Honest to God, Al, Mike was late at work and I couldn't get a babysitter at the last minute. I rang Mary and asked her to hold your hand.'

'Held me by the balls, more like.'

'I thought she might boost your confidence.'

'Huh! She booted it into touch.'

I asked her if she'd heard from Megan. I'd called her a couple of times to tell her about New York but just got voicemail and no call back.

'No, she seems to have gone to ground. Apparently she's staying away from the usual haunts. It's odd. But she knows you're going.'

The day before my flight I borrowed Nick's car and took most of my stuff up to Taff's Well for storage. Mam and Dad sat in the kitchen with me, drinking tea and looking as if I'd been given a few months to live.

'It's only for a year,' I said. 'And I'll be back for Christmas.'

'What about Megan?' asked Mam.

'She doesn't want to talk to me,' I said. 'Has she been in touch with you?'

'No,' said Mam.

I thought that was just plain bloody-minded of her, given how fond they both were of her. I'd written her quite a long letter, saying that this might just be the break we needed - could we meet when I came back to see if there was a chance we might get back together? I was prepared to give it another go if she was. Needless to say, there was no reply.

Chapter Four

From the outside, The Wayside Inn did indeed look like three similar but distinct red brick town houses, with tall sash windows and a huge bay in the middle one. Inside it was an hotchpotch of decors and furniture which added up to a pleasing whole, all wood paneling and steps and stairs. I'd booked a room for a month. An elderly receptionist checked me in with a warm welcome. It was all very cosy.

My room was on the third floor of the third house along, looking out onto the street through old-fashioned, wooden louvred shutters, which would spread the light at different angles as you opened and shut various parts of them. It had a Victorian feel, with a solid oak chest of drawers, a four-poster bed and, in the window, a long, low-backed couch in the classical style. Rugs were scattered on the pine floorboards, and there was a large white wooden fireplace surrounding a red brick grate. Up a step, the bathroom was built into a kind of antechamber, with no door but a tiled wall curving around a massive claw-toed bath underneath a copper shower head the size of small umbrella. Back in the room, electrified brass lamps and a ceiling fan completed the picture, and in the corner, a Chippendale secretaire on which I wrote this description.

For the first time in weeks I sensed a glimmer of hope, the possibility of adventure. I was starting on a new journey, even if my steps were faltering and fearful. I'd had several pieces of advice about what do to when you're really low:

1) Start keeping a diary

2) Clean something - preferably windows

3) Do something - take up a hobby

4) Throw away things you no longer need - clothes, habits, people etc

5) Make your bed every morning.

Well, at least I'd made a start on number 1). And looking round at the room, I did at least feel a vague sense of well-being for the first time in weeks. Number 4) had largely been taken care of by Megan and the move. Number 5) was no big effort, since making the bed merely entailed throwing back the duvet, or comforter as the Americans called them, and then the chambermaid remade it anyway. Numbers 2) and 3) would have to wait.

I'm sorry to note that fleeting sense of well-being didn't last very long. After I'd unpacked I sat on the bed wondering what to do next. I didn't know a soul in New York, and had only been there a couple of times on short breaks, one of which I'd organised as a surprise for Megan for our fifth wedding anniversary. She seemed delighted at the time, but clearly it was another piece of evidence of my controlling behaviour. Tyler had given me the numbers of some good friends and urged me to call them when I got there, but I couldn't face it. I wandered out into the streets. The evening ahead of me stretched long.

Greenwich Village was nice enough, with its off-beat, old world charm, an oasis in the canyons of New York. I briefly considered strolling up to the Empire State or somewhere for form's sake, but my heart wasn't in it. I ended up having dinner in a diner on the corner, almost deserted like that Hopper painting, *Nighthawks* I seemed to remember it was called. It didn't even have that vague sense of expectancy that lurk behind his pictures, and did nothing to enhance my mood. I went back and tried to read myself to sleep, which wasn't easy, even with jet lag on my side.

Things did pick up slightly in the next few days, when I could focus on starting classes at Stuyvesant. I'd mugged up on American media as much as I could and had become addicted to The New York Times, which I found infinitely better than anything Britain had to offer. I made my way by subway up to the sprawling campus on the Upper West Side, and then to one of its many red brick, neo-Georgian buildings which housed my faculty. I met the Head of School. She was anything but the caricature I now realise I'd formed subconsciously: tall, bearded, wearing horn-rimmed glasses and one of those spotted bow ties which only American professors seem to wear any more. Vanessa was tiny, she could have been not much more than five feet tall, with hennaed hair in a bob and a somewhat hippyish get-up.

Her opening gambit surprised me somewhat.

'I have Welsh ancestry, you know. Do I look Welsh?'

I'd have put her down as Italian if anything but didn't want to disappoint her.

'Well, you're tiny. That's a start.'

'The Welsh are small?'

'Yes, we had to fit down the mines.'

She laughed.

'One of my favourite films is *How Green Was My Valley*. Do the miners really come home singing like that?'

'There aren't any miners in Wales anymore. Thatcher saw to that.'

I expected a more thorough walk through learning aims, outcomes, teaching methods and so on, but the short conversation continued in the same chatty vein. I thought we would get on just fine.

Luckily enough, my first lecture the next day was one I'd taught in Cardiff: History and Ideas, to the second years or 'sophomores' as they're rather pretentiously called in the US. (Had to look it up. It comes from the Greek and means 'wise fools.'). People find it surprising and even amusing that we teach students different ways of perceiving the world and so study the philosophies of Marx, Durkheim, Bourdieu and the like. It's a world they have to report on, after all, and interpret. As Bourdieu said, we bring our own prejudices to the discipline without even realising it.

The students on the whole were more eager and engaged than their Welsh counterparts. I found them a bewildering mix of formal and casual, worldly and naive, questioning yet gullible. But they were welcoming and there was none of the 'too cool for school' attitude I'd come to expect. Many of them were more smartly dressed too, but my rumpled clothes and unkempt hair were not too out of place. The lecture theatre was one of those banked rows of seats affairs, which I don't like because my natural style is to wander among the students during class, working the floor. There were many questions, which to me is always a good sign, and at the end the usual clutch came up to the podium to ask me more. One guy, who looked about 35 and wore a sports jacket several sizes too small for him, said, 'That was great. You guys could talk crap and it still comes out sounding like Shakespeare.' I chose to take this as a compliment. As I walked out behind them, I found Vanessa waiting in the corridor.

'Are you checking on me,' I asked, somewhat aggressively it now appears.

'Just came to see if you were OK. You'll be fine.'

'How do you know?'

'There was a buzz as they came out of the room. They were interested in the class. They liked you. I can tell.'

I liked that about Vanessa. Decisive, no-nonsense.

Much as I felt at home in The Wayside Inn, my budget soon forced me to look elsewhere. I found a fourth-floor apartment in the East Village, small even by New York standards, with a living room and galley kitchen, shower-room, and bedroom which in this case meant there was room for a bed and little else. The two windows looked out to the back, onto a jumble of minute gardens, patios and decks, like the set of Hitchcock's *Rear Window*.

It suited my mood. Minimal, functional, get through the day. I even cleaned the windows, working through my checklist of ways to cheer up, and it worked for a day or two. I made an effort to put the place in order with my meagre belongings. It's amazing how quickly a place can become a home, of sorts. A photograph placed casually on a shelf can soon make its home there and not look right anywhere else. At times I would catch myself finding joy in the simplest of things, like the plants in a window box opposite dancing in the breeze. I began to notice and find some solace in the strange minutiae of New York life – the steaming manholes in cold, wet streets; the cartoon mailboxes, as I thought of them; those odd, almost mediaeval round wooden water towers on top of old buildings.

Or was I going mad? This possibility had become a preoccupation.

The moments of respite, as welcome as they were, remained fleeting, and I often thought that I was losing it. Things started to feel less and less real, even very solid things like the banister going up to my apartment. It was as if it melted away when I put my hand on it to haul myself up the stairs. The point of doing even the most basic things like eating would suddenly slip beyond my grasp.

I needed something to get me out of myself, to save me from evenings alone in the apartment or a nearby bar. I was in danger of finding solace in the bottom of a glass, and women didn't seem to interest me much any more. It was Nick who wrote and gave me the third piece of advice: 'When you're feeling like this, it's time to get out of the house and do something.' Nick, I remembered now, had been through something similar a couple of years ago. My unconsidered way of helping him was to pat him on the back, tell him to buck up and buy him another pint. In my self-absorption I'd failed even to register this when he took me in.

He was right. I was festering. I'd only been in the place a month but it was now a pigsty, however tiny a pigsty. The sink was brimming with unwashed plates and mouldy mugs. The bed was strewn with smelly clothes and underneath the white sheets had turned grey. The living room was carpeted with pizza boxes, some still containing a dried slice or two, crushed beer cans and overflowing ashtrays. I just had to think of what I could get out of the house and do. It was Kath who suggested Bridge again, on the phone one rainy Sunday afternoon.

'Why don't you join a club? You know you enjoy it when you make the effort'

'Are you kidding? Scary Mary scarred me for life.'

'Oh, get back on your horse and drink your milk.'

I didn't take it seriously at first, but her words kept coming back to me. I knew that the American system was different from the British one. I bought a book - *Commonsense Bidding* by William S Root - and worked my way through the bewildering algorithms of Standard American. It was full of strange-sounding conventions like Landy, Leaping Michaels and Jacoby Transfers. Hard to see that they were either sensible or common. These I did my best to ignore for the time being and ploughed on with the basics. The differences were small but could be crucial, not unlike the nuances involved in teaching journalism in another country. The fundamentals are there, the niceties have to be learnt. In Standard American Yellow Card, to give the system its full name, you don't open the bidding in a Spade or Heart unless you have at least five cards in that suit. This is known as Five-card Majors. In the British system, Acol, named after the road in Hampstead where it was invented, you can open with four. If you open with 1NT in SAYC, it means you've got between fifteen to seventeen points and an even distribution of the suits. In Acol, it promises only twelve to fourteen points. If you don't adapt you're giving the wrong information to your partner.

And then there are the many conventions - bids which mean specific things and have exotic names. Stayman, for example. If your partner opens 1NT, and you want to find out if they have a four-card major, you reply 2C. This doesn't mean you want to play in clubs, it's just asking your partner to bid hearts or spades if they've got four of them. Clearly, if this goes wrong it spells disaster. By the end of the book, I needed a lie down with a stiff drink.

So it was with some trepidation that I started looking for Bridge clubs. I didn't know where to start so I tried the phone book. There were quite a few listed, somewhat to my surprise. One was fairly near the University, up on Amsterdam Avenue. It was called the New Cavendish, which I thought sounded clubby and off-putting. I pictured wooden panels and leather chairs.

It was still a couple of days before I could bring myself to pick up the phone. I'd finally tackled my Augean Stables and cleaning was not quite the Herculean task I'd imagined it would be. A couple of trips to the launderette, a couple of bin bags of rubbish and a good session at the sink one evening broke the back of it. The next afternoon I got home from classes fairly early. I set to with the cleaning stuff. Because it was so small I'd finished the whole place in no time. I stood in the middle of the room looking around me with a great sense of achievement, and of surprise that the cloud that had been hanging over me could be so quickly dispersed. I felt cleansed myself. I think it was a Thursday night (there was no note of it my diary). Afterwards I sat down in the leather armchair and noticed I was drumming my fingers on the arm. I didn't want to go on another lonely bar hop.

I dialled the number for the New Cavendish, little knowing what I was letting myself in for, that it was one of the foremost clubs in New York. I didn't even know what to expect from the call, or even what to ask for.

'New Cavendish', said a gentle man's voice.

'Ah, hello. My name's Al. I'm looking for a game', thinking as I said it that it sounded more like a request for an all-night poker session in a back alley bar.

'Well, have you played club bridge before?' asked the gentle voice.

'Oh, yes, in the United Kingdom', I said, as airily as I could.

'What level are you?'

'Intermediate?' I hazarded, recalling a phrase I read in the book.

'Tuesdays and Fridays would suit you best'. He sounded as if he was busy and wanted to get off the line.

'What about a partner?'

'Come along about half an hour before the start of the game and I'll find a partner for you. Come at seven and ask for me, Clarke.'

'Oh, well, thanks. So shall we say tomorrow?'

'We shall. Bye.'

That was easy. Too easy perhaps. As I put down the phone I felt a tinge of nervousness - an emotion, I supposed, to be welcomed after weeks of emptiness. Nerves after all were a sign that you cared about something, weren't they? And I thought I was past caring.

The next morning I got up feeling better than I'd done in a long while, and made my bed straightaway. I had my coffee and cereal leaning against the sink and looking out of the window. It was more breakfast than I'd had in ages too. I wondered how long it would last. And if I'd have the nerve to go through with it that night.

My classes finished at five and I had two or three hours to fill.

I worked in the library for a couple of them, preparing for the next week. Then I ambled down the few blocks to W 86th Street, stopping for a cup of coffee on the way. It was my second cup that day, more than I usually drink but I didn't want to risk the Dutch courage of a couple of beers before the club in case it backfired. I found ordering a coffee in New York something of a trial because the choices were so bewildering, and you were meant to reel them off automatically. As I couldn't, the guy had to prompt me for every choice which took ages. He clearly found my accent difficult to follow, and this prolonged the rigmarole. I almost snapped, 'Just gimme the goddam coffee' half-way through but managed to keep what little cool I had left.

I found the address easily enough. It was rather a shabby sixties office block. The directory of brass plates in the lobby indicated the third floor. By now I'd got used to subtracting a floor from Americans directions, as they start counting One from the Ground Floor. I took the rickety elevator, followed the signs to the suite number, swallowed and entered. It was like being the new boy at school, or in those nightmares I still had of turning up to an exam without doing any revision, and often without any trousers.

No-one took the slightest bit of notice of me. They were standing or sitting around in small groups, chatting, checking scores on the notice boards, getting coffee and cookies from the little kitchen off to the side of the room. They reminded me of the Pontcanna players; mainly elderly, rather superior and not over-attentive to their looks or dress, especially the men.

The place had a familiar ring to it too. Not quite the wooden paneling I'd imagined but that laminated stuff so fake you wonder why it bothers. It was bigger than the room in The Blue Angel of course, with two rows of about twenty tables covered in the green baize. Each one had the same red plastic bidding boxes and the metal card trays in the centre.

I asked a woman reading a sheet of paper on the notice board where Clarke was. She pointed to a thin, rather nervous guy with big glasses who was doing something with the metal trays. He could have been a maths teacher. Someone else went up to ask him a question and he had a way of doing a little sideways dance and scratching behind his ear like a nervous pup. He made me feel more relaxed straight away.

When the woman had finished with him I went up and said, 'Hello, Clarke? I'm Al, the new boy. I rang yesterday'.

'Oh, uh, yes. Ah, hello'. I'd learn that Clarke's economical conversation was liberally sprinkled with uhs and ahs. He shook hands formally and I decided I liked him.

He found me a partner but I can't remember who it was now. I've checked my diary but again it makes no mention. It records 'Played Bridge at the New Cavendish. Enjoyed myself for the first time in a long time'. They're pretty funny things, diaries. Or at least mine is, reading it back: the things that are in it, and the things that are not. It's usually hard to judge the significance of the moment, the everyday events that will affect the rest of your life.

It didn't even record meeting Greta, although I know I did later that night. Whoever my partner was, we were playing East/West, which meant we moved on a table after every four hands, or boards as they're called. I think I more or less held my own, as panic-striking as it was at times. Not too many egregious gaffes, although I had to keep concentrating to avoid opening a major suit (hearts or spades) with just four cards. I came close to it.

I learnt as I went along. Everything moved like clockwork and no delay was tolerated. Most people were brusque but informative, but others would glare at you if you hesitated for more than a few seconds over your bid or the play. I found that people here really only cared about the major suits or No Trump - the minors hardly counted. A major was the suit to open with. If you didn't have five cards in either suit, the next preference would be 1NT, if you had fifteen to seventeen points and an even distribution of cards (quite a precise bid, as you can see). The last resort would be to open IC. It doesn't even promise good clubs, necessarily. It's saying, 'I have enough points to open, no five-card major, and not enough points for INT.' This is known as a Short Club. Not to be confused with opening 2C, one of the strongest opening bids you can make. A minefield. And I still found the bidding boxes fiddly. It was easy to pull out the wrong card.

It was the custom at the New Cavendish to hang around after the game for the fifteen minutes or so it took Clarke to put the scores in the computer. He'd post the results on a printout on the notice board. I was relieved to find we hadn't come last, although I don't think we were far off. But at least it gave me some encouragement to come again. It had indeed taken me out of myself. I would almost say enjoyed myself. Well, I did, in the diary.

Oh, yes. Greta. I remember I played against her on the last table. She was sitting in the North position in the chair nearest the door. I didn't even notice her at first. But then she made what to me was an unusual bid. Her partner opened 1S, my partner passed, and she jumped straight to 4S, straight to game. I asked her what she meant. She turned her head very slightly and slowly towards me, like a spooky ventriloquist's dummy. She stared at me icily. I stared back. It would be difficult to guess her age. She was one of those impeccably preserved elderly women, her made-up face framed with shiny silver hair. She wore a black turtleneck, an expensive silk scarf pinned to it with a huge gold broach.

'Don't you know you should ask my partner for an explanation, not me?'

I did vaguely recall this rule of etiquette. I looked at her partner.

'It's when…..' she flustered, and looked at Greta.

'She opened 1S and I have a fistful of them,' said Greta impatiently, breaking the very rule she accused me of not obeying a moment ago. 'I'm too strong to reply 2S and too weak to go 3S - so I go straight to game. Get the picture now?'

'Yes, thank you'.

'Enjoy the free lesson?'

I gave her a smile and looked for one from her. There was none. What an unpleasant old woman, I remember thinking, I hope I never have to play with her again.

Chapter Five

I do know that the first time I played with Greta was the next Friday. This time my diary didn't let me down, although it did confine itself to: 'In the evening to New Cavendish and played with a rather strange woman called Greta. Managed to avert another disaster'.

But I see the evening perfectly well in my mind's eye. I did have qualms in the week about going back there. Yes, I'd enjoyed it in a masochistic, competitive way. But back in my normal routine it all seemed unreal. These people were not of my world and I was out of their league. I would never be able to play like them, become one of them, and nor would I want to. And I knew that these little new-found enthusiasms were apt to be temporary.

It was Nick who encouraged me to persist. It's worth coming through the other side, he said when I spoke to him on the phone. And this time I knew he knew what he was talking about. When I got there the next Friday I found Clarke and said I needed a partner again.

'Uh, yeah, you could, ah, play with Greta, I guess,' he offered - somewhat warily, I thought, looking at me sideways through the corner of his eyes. He seemed relieved when my reaction was nothing stronger than a smile and raised eyebrows, suggesting I'd go along with whatever he said.

He ushered me back over to the door with that little sideways shuffle of his. It was only when we got to the table that I remembered Greta was that rude old woman I hoped I'd never have to partner. There she was, enthroned in her chair nearest the door, hands folded on the table in front of her. She was surveying the room regally, not quite masking a girlish look of expectation. Clarke uhed and ahed the introduction, and she eyed me acidly. I couldn't back out now.

'Back for more free lessons?' she enquired, and this time I thought I did detect a faint twinkle of amusement in her eyes. It was a crisp, articulate voice, young in a way, just edged with the crackle of old age. I volunteered rather hesitantly that I was a fairly inexperienced player and would be very grateful if she could take me by the hand. She gave a slight bow as if bestowing me a great favour and indicated the chair opposite with her outstretched hand. I would learn that a little old-fashioned courtesy went a long way with Greta.

'I don't play anything fancy,' she said as I sat down. I said that was fine with me. We ran through the conventions we would play. I was relieved to find I knew most of them, and we agreed on the ones I did. No Leaping Michaels. As we waited for our East and West to take their place, I could see her appraising me thoughtfully.

'You're English,' she asserted.

'Welsh,' I corrected.

'Ah, Welsh,' she nodded with her head tilted to one side, as if to say she knew all about that. 'I'm from Europe myself, originally.' Jewish, I decided. I pictured her arriving in New York on the eve of war, a smart young woman in a fur coat and a funny hat.

East and West duly sat down and we began, a little shakily at first, Greta and I. A couple of times I slipped back into opening 1NT with twelve to fourteen points, forgetting about the Short Club. Even though catastrophe was kept at bay, Greta would reward me with a withering look and a little lecture after the hand was played. I gave an apologetic shrug and explained we open a weak No Trump in the British system.

'Oh, you have your own system?' she accused, as though it were a daft idea and we only had ourselves to blame.

I explained we played four-card majors, a weak No Trump, and minor bids were natural.

'Oh, that's no use at all. Don't waste your time on the minors. What's your system called?'

'Acol. I think it's the name of the road in London where it was first played.'

She looked a little mollified and intrigued, a smile struggling with the corners of her mouth.

'Well, forget about it. It's only the majors and No Trump that matter'.

In a while though we began to get into our stride. Greta was indeed a straightforward but very solid player - just what I needed - and we sort of clicked. I could almost sense where her bidding was leading, what she was aiming for, and this needless to say is a very good thing to have in a partnership. I have to confess that I could also read her face quite well, subtle though her expressions were. Any kind of communication of this sort would be frowned on officially of course, but it was nothing anyone else could detect or object to. If she liked my bid a certain impassive satisfaction would appear on her face. Otherwise, an almost imperceptible frown.

We made some good contracts that night, and, the cards being with Greta, she played and made them, calling for the cards from me in dummy with a calm, assured deliberation, lost in concentration.

Next to cards, it quickly became plain that Greta's other chief source of amusement was being staggeringly rude to the opponents as they came and went at our table. One unfortunate balding man, whom I suspect had not before encountered her, had the habit of scratching his head while mulling over his bid. Greta quickly upbraided him.

'How rude of you to scratch your head at the table,' she bellowed. 'Don't you realise you're dropping bits of sweat and skin all over the place?' That was Greta, a strange mix of the ethereal and the earthy.

The man stared at her open-mouthed, utterly incapable of reply, and glanced nervously at his partner and me. He went to pieces after that. I found myself wondering if this was a tactic on Greta's part.

His partner was Lily, the polar opposite of Greta in every way. She was a dance teacher from Brooklyn, I learned later. She must have been about sixty, wore a sequinned sweater and had jet-black, gypsy-style hair. She evidently *had* met Greta before, and was standing for none of her nonsense. She stared at her, chewing gum noisily.

Lily turned to me. 'One more crack like that and I'll smack her in the kisser,' she said just as loudly.

I glanced at Greta, who was looking around her serenely, as if she hadn't heard. But she must have. Eventually she turned to Lily and demanded:

'Must you chew your gum so loudly?'

'Yes,' snapped back Lily, 'I must,' and gave a couple of particularly animalistic chews in front of her face. 'It relieves the stress caused by rude people'.

She fairly shouted out those last two words, then looked back at me with a conspiratorial smile, clearly calculating that this would serve to antagonise Greta even further.

But Greta looked away, sensing perhaps that Lily was a good match for her. Instead, she turned her attention back to Lily's partner, the little balding man, still cowering after her earlier onslaught. As we picked up our cards in the fourth and final game of this fraught foursome, he was holding his cards too far away from him. This is considered bad form, as opponents can inadvertently, or advertently for that matter, glimpse the cards.

'Chest your cards!' commanded Greta sharply, making the little bald man jump visibly.

'Or tit your stack, as we say in my neck of the woods', said Lily to me with a mischievous grin, delighted at this chance to be vulgar in front of Greta. 'There's no need to be so upty-topty.' Again, though, Greta made a point of looking round the room unperturbed, although her lips were pursed.

After they moved on I felt oddly guilty for enjoying Lily's spirited combat with Greta, as if I'd been disloyal to her, or at least that that's how she'd view it. And indeed she did. I tried to strike up casual conversation again, but she'd give me only the curtest of replies. And she seemed to make the next opponents suffer even more, so that in the end I was dreading the approach of each new pair, stepping smiling and innocent towards humiliation.

It was something of a relief when it was over, although I couldn't really pretend not to have enjoyed it. Greta made no move to go, so I sat there with her in silence, waiting for the results. When Clarke came and pinned the printout on the green felt notice board, Greta spoke at last.

'Go, quick, before it gets too crowded.'

I obeyed, but as I towered above most of the oldies anyway I had no trouble seeing that we'd come about middle – seventeenth or eighteenth of the forty or so pairs. I was exhilarated, but doubted Greta would be.

'Well, we can do better next time,' she said, refusing my hand as she struggled out of her chair. She walked with a stick, which hung on the back of it. It was only when I got outside in the rain, running for the subway, that I wondered if that meant we had a date for next Friday, and I wondered what I thought about that.

In the intervening week I did, I suppose, give it a second or even third thought. Why did I want to be stuck with an old bat like that, when I should be seeking out youthful drive and verve to help me out of my myopic misery? On the other hand I did feel comfortable playing with her, there was the click, and she seemed to tolerate me slightly better than she did most others.

Without coming to any conscious decision, I found myself ringing the buzzer at the New Cavendish the next Friday and walking in about fifteen minutes before kick-off. Even before I entered the main room I could see her head - the helmet of hair silvery in colour and filigree - slowly turning around, surveying the room like something mechanical. I sauntered up to her, trying to be casual. She gave me a Where've You Been? look, and the merest of nods, which seemed to serve both as hello and an invitation to sit down. But I was taking no chances - she did scare me a little.

'OK if I sit here?' I smiled.

'Why not?' she said dryly, as if wishing she could think of a valid reason.

So I sat down, and she thawed a little as we made desultory remarks back and fore. As we did, it became clear that her initial frostiness was due to her belief that I had forgotten about our date. She was cross because I asked her if I could sit down. She thought we had an understanding. I explained it in terms of British over-politeness, which seemed to satisfy her, and we moved on.

As the play got going, we built on the fairly solid start we'd made the week before. I bandied about Short Club and strong No Trump bids like a native. We barely put a foot wrong, in the bidding or the playing. We had quite a few 3NT contracts, which seemed to be our forte, our natural inclination if we had the right cards. This meant you had to make nine of the possible thirteen tricks, and was the cheapest contract to get you to a game score. You needed to make four hearts or spades to reach that score, and five in the minor suits of clubs and diamonds. Greta was so absorbed that she even behaved herself quite well with the opponents. Barely a rude remark escaped her lips.

At the end she seemed pleased with the way things had gone. We sat there at the table, the two of us, waiting for Clarke to pin up the results. From time to time Greta drummed her fingers lightly on the green baize of the table. Clarke thrust his way through the usual small, determined gaggle which enveloped him as he made his way to the notice board with the flimsy piece of paper.

Greta didn't need to prompt me this time. I moved as fast as dignity allowed. At first I couldn't find our names, but as I scanned upwards I could see them in third place. My eyes lingered on them a while, checking I hadn't made a mistake and enjoying it.

'Third,' I mouthed to Greta as I walked back towards her, and held up three fingers.

She was so delighted she positively beamed.

'I guess you won't have second thoughts about playing with me next week, huh?'

I laughed, and agreed we'd definitely play next Friday. But we swapped phone numbers just in case.

And so we fell into a regular pattern of Friday night dates, Greta and I. But I soon learnt that she would expect a confirming phone call sometime late Friday afternoon. If I didn't call and just turned up at the club, she would sulk and for a while make a vague pretence that she might be playing with someone else if they showed up. I'd have to skulk around the table like a naughty schoolboy until she beckoned me begrudgingly to the empty chair opposite her.

Before long I discovered that there were sessions on Tuesdays which were a little more my level. Clarke gave a little lesson beforehand. Greta very rarely went any evening except Friday, but soon I had enough confidence to go alone on the Tuesday a couple of times and enjoyed it.

The lessons filled in the gaps between what Greta taught me almost intuitively and the science behind the strategy. Clarke would chalk up hands on the blackboard and invite us to suggest bids or play. There was a theme to each lesson - leads, discards, signalling and so on. The high-low signal for example: if you have just two cards in a suit (a doubleton) you can let your partner know this by playing the higher card first and then the lower, so your partner knows you now have a void in that suit and can trump them next time round. In other circumstances, if your partner is winning a trick - let's say in diamonds when hearts are trumps, you can tell him what suit you'd like him to lead next. If you put on a high diamond (seven and above) it means you'd like the next suit up apart from trumps, so in this case it's saying, 'Lead a spade please.' If you put on a low diamond, it's asking for a club. Neat, huh? Of course this doesn't always work in practice as you might only have diamonds under seven when you want spades.

On Tuesdays I fell in to partnering Marco, a somewhat scabrous yet charismatic music journalist. I'd seen him a couple of times on Friday too. He didn't say very much - seemed to turn up just for the game, not the socialising, such as it was, and didn't even wait for the scores afterwards. New Cavendish players on the whole were a self-contained, closed bunch, polite enough but not exactly welcoming or even very curious about newcomers.

Gradually, though, I started to get to know a few of the friendlier ones. There was one young woman who introduced herself as Panda. The next time she came to sit at our table, I said, 'It's Panda, isn't it?'

'You remembered!' she cried, her voice full of pleased surprise.

As she did so, Greta showed every sign of possessiveness. She ignored her warm smile, and turned her shoulder to her. She soon caught wind of the fact that I was playing with Marco on Tuesdays.

'Whatchya want to play with him for?' she demanded as we were waiting for the next game to start.

'He's OK. Just turns up for the game. It's good practice for me. And Clarke gives a little lesson beforehand. It makes me see things more clearly'.

Greta harrumphed. I'd always liked that word but never knew precisely what it meant. Yet I knew that what Greta was doing was harrumphing.

'Clarke! What can he teach you?' The words, 'that I can't' hung unspoken between us. I mentioned the high-low signal for a doubleton.

'Oh yes, we can do that,' she said, as if granting a mundane wish to a small child.

If there was someone I paid particular attention to, without even realising it, Greta would stick her oar in.

'She thinks she's the cat's miaow', she said of so-and-so (they were usually female), whom Greta thought had been overly friendly.

'Do you say cat's miaow in Britain?' she asked, maybe seeing my forehead crinkle into a question mark.

'No. Bee's knees,' I said, realising a little too late as usual that she'd once again drawn me into her trap of complicity, the two of us against everyone else. 'We say "She thinks she's the bee's knees".'

Greta was delighted. 'Do bees have knees?' she mused, with her lips pursed. 'Yes, I suppose they do. The bee's knees. She thinks she's the bee's knees.' She played around with the phrase.

I got chatting to a tall, quiet lecturer in French literature at another university. She was in her fifties I would say. I forget her name now. She seemed to like discussing French novels, old and new, with me, although obviously I was not in her league at all.

'You like her, don't you?' accused Greta one time before the poor woman had barely left the table.

'Greta!' I warned.

'Well, she drinks.' She must have heard.

'How do you know she drinks?' I hissed when I was sure she was out of earshot.

'You can smell it. Can't you smell it?'

I couldn't smell a thing. She must be making it up. I was never quite sure if she was aware of how nasty she was being, let alone regretted it, but often when she'd behaved particularly badly she'd make some gesture the following Friday.

'I went to Temple today,' she'd say conversationally, waiting for our first opponents to take their place. I'd be angry with her and maybe not answer straightaway. 'I know you're not of my faith, but I prayed for you.'

I wouldn't know how to respond to such a gambit, or even if I wanted to, but she could always find a way of snapping you out of your sulk and make me say something. 'That's very nice of you,' I'd sniff.

It didn't really occur to me to wonder what the others made of this odd relationship until one evening after a particularly long harangue against a man who talked during play. His partner, a kind, witty woman, sidled up to me while we were waiting for the scores.

'How's it going?' she asked with a smile and a sidelong glance back at Greta at the table.

'Oh good, thanks.' I'd learnt to upgrade my usual 'Fine' - not nearly positive enough for Americans.

'You know, if ever you want a change of partner, you know, I have a nephew who's keen to play, and he's looking for someone……'

She looked back at Greta again and I knew what she meant.

'Oh, thanks. I…..well, I'll let you know. I'm doing OK with Greta.'

She looked at me, uncomprehending.

'For the time being, at least,' I added.

She managed a smile.

'Oh well, if you change your mind…..' Again she left the sentence hanging.

'I'll let you know.' She looked disappointed.

The truth is, I suspect, I was sorry for Greta. She had a way of hooking me to her somehow, seconding me as her only ally against a hostile world. I was still sorry for myself too. But bit by bit, without my fully realising it - let alone analysing it - she was bringing back some sense of purpose in my life, something almost to look forward to again. At the time I really didn't foresee any problems with the arrangement. And for some reason, on my way back down on the subway I thought of that Woody Allen quote: 'Having sex is like playing Bridge. If you don't have a good partner you'd better have a good hand.'

Chapter Six

It was at this time - and here my sketchy diary is of help, providing times and dates - that I began seeing someone from the faculty. She wasn't a student exactly. She was doing research into social housing in New York City, so I didn't have any qualms about dereliction of duty. She was only four or five years younger than me. I'd noticed her around the building. She was strikingly blond and vivacious, with a bright, winning smile but sad eyes. It started slowly, with just a coffee together in the cafeteria. She wanted to know about social housing in Britain, and I was able to chat to her about council estates in a general, anecdotal way. But just as things were in danger of getting a little too worthy, she'd inject some of her wry humour into the proceedings. We got round to talking about Broadway theatre, and she told me she been to see a production of Anne Frank the musical, with the blonde starlet Pia Zadora improbably cast in the title role.

'She was so bad that when the Nazis raided her house someone in the front row shouted out "She's in the attic!" '

That made me laugh like I hadn't for weeks, and it was a strange sound, an echo of the past. Another thing I liked about Ewa (pronounced Eh-va as she was always quick to point out - Polish) was that she could come across as quite prim and aloof, but had a mouth on her, as my mother would say. Every now and then she came out with something that would make a fishwife blush. One coffee led to another, then a drink, and a couple of weeks later I asked her out to dinner. I was quite surprised when she said yes.

We went to a cosy Italian not far from my apartment in the Village. I found her intriguing, her sad eyes behind the smile, a certain reserve behind her easy-going manner. The conversation was easy. Gradually, with the candlelight and wine, I found my libido making a comeback. Before I knew it, in the time-honoured euphemism, I was asking her back for coffee. She nodded in a mock-prim kind of way.

We didn't bother with the coffee. I opened some more wine to calm my nerves. She just nursed hers. It was twelve years or more since I'd done anything like that, and I was apprehensive. I feared I'd lost my knack. I even considered explaining I'd split up from my wife and was a bit out of practice, but stopped myself in time. Hardly the most romantic invitation into the boudoir.

I have to confess it wasn't a spectacular start on my part, but she was patient and knew how to relax me. I think at one point I did mumble something about not having done this for quite a while, but she didn't seem to mind. In fact it seemed to soften her a little. She wanted to know why I'd been alone. I told her, and as I talked things started working.

I don't think either of us would have said we were dating, exactly. The sex was casual but good, after that shaky start on my part. Ewa didn't seem to want any ties any more than I did. But apart from that I began to enjoy going out again, other than just to the New Cavendish and a few local bars.

Ewa's idea of going out was usually linked with her work in some way, but it was fun. She was recording what she called living history - people's stories about their lives when they first came to New York. When I told her I wanted to climb the Statue of Liberty, she suggested we also took in the museum on Ellis Island nearby, where hundreds of thousands of immigrants were processed around the turn of the century. It was a good suggestion.

Climbing up the stairs inside the statue was slow and claustrophobic, and the crush in the crown at the top barely gave you the chance to appreciate the stunning views through the tiny windows. But I found the Ellis Island museum fascinating. On maps on the walls huge arrows tracked the influx from various troubled parts of the world. Slabs of text next to them gave statistics and context. And it struck me there, in the vast, stark hall, how little I really understood about America: where its values and valours came from, what made it great indeed. Like most Brits I'd assumed I knew quite a bit about America, through screens big and small, music and celebrity. Easy to knock, hard to know. Uncle Sam as the world's Aunt Sally.

What hit me on Ellis Island was the fear and hope that built a nation, in times our great-great grandparents would remember. Fear had driven millions from economic, political or religious oppression, often in what was the considered the civilised world. In packed steamers from Liverpool or Naples, Hamburg or Dublin millions left their hearth and kin with little more than their fare and the clothes they wore, to take a chance on the unknown, and the hope of something better.

The stinking, festering steerage below decks were a tragic, living embodiment of the survival of the fittest, with the young, old, sick or weak often succumbing on the Atlantic. I imagined the survivors' first sighting of the Statue of Liberty, when they could venture on deck after weeks in those fearful conditions, unable to read the promise on the book in her hand: 'Give me the poor, huddled masses.......' I suppose I knew all this in a vague kind of way, but I'd never really felt it. It made my little exile seem like a holiday by comparison. I said as much to Ewa - by now I'd heard quite a bit about her family coming from Poland - and I think it pleased her to see how moved I was.

We progressed slowly through the great hall, as they would have done, at once relieved and grieving maybe for those they left behind or who didn't make it. We passed the place where they'd have undergone undignified medical exams by officious officials who'd peremptorily approximate their name to the nearest Anglicisation, and came to the Kissing Point, where lucky loved ones were reunited. I was hungry for more stories about what happened to them then.

The next Saturday Ewa showed me another facet of the immigration story. She took me to the Lower East Side Tenement Museum (appointment only). It was in a street that had hardly been touched by the modern world of Manhattan, lined with red brick houses clad with iron fire escapes. Ewa said it was typical of the kind of place where people off the boats would end up. The Museum itself was a perfectly-preserved tenement block. Even the smell was preserved, the smell of overcrowding and poverty.

We visited a flat on the third floor, I think it was, which was a series of three small rooms backing off the one which overlooked the street. In between each was a window in the wall to let through the light, and the third looked out to a grimy, gloomy shaft which let in the most meagre gleams of daylight.

The water closets were lined up on the landing, five or six wooden doors with holes drilled in them for some kind of ventilation. The rooms were empty save for a tin trunk underneath the back window which looked into that thin, dirty shaft. The guide played a tape to the six or seven of us traipsing around. It was the voice of a woman who'd lived there as a little girl with her large Italian family. I pictured her now as an elderly middle-class matron living in New Jersey or somewhere. She recalled those days with a mix of warmth and wonderment that she could have survived what to me seemed such atrocious conditions. Yet then it was simply her home.

She related how the tin trunk by the window was her stage, where she and her brother put on shows for the family. And on Fridays a basket would be lowered down the shaft by Mrs Liebewitz who lived a couple of floors above, old and alone. Mrs Liebewitz didn't go out much, and on the Jewish Sabbath didn't go out at all. So she'd lower her basket with a note for the little girl with a message and the right amount of change saying, 'Please get me a loaf of bread and a bottle of milk'. The little girl would skip off on her errand, place the shopping in the basket and watch it being winched slowly up again.

All this was narrated in a clear, unemotional, matter of fact manner which made it all the more moving. Ewa then revealed she'd tracked her down herself and recorded the story as part of her research. This was the tape the Museum used. She lived in Palisades - not quite in New Jersey but as near as dammit - just over the state line in New York. The family name was Ferrante and they'd come from Sicily. The little girl's name was Alice (sounds wonderful pronounced the Italian way - A-lee-chay. Never mind that it means anchovy). She married and became a drama teacher in public schools. As Ewa explained all this to me, I fully understood perhaps for the first time, what Ewa's living history thing was all about, how the stories of ordinary people can bring dusty history books to life. I was impressed, all the more that she told me all this in an almost bashful fashion. I felt even closer to her.

I wandered back into the front room and noticed there were some artefacts after all: two old-fashioned, heavy-framed pictures on the wall of a stiff, buttoned-up Victorian couple, their wrinkled faces hard and careworn. They would have been the grandparents, I would have thought, of the little girl on the tin trunk. I wondered if they made the journey too, and passed through Ellis Island. And why their portraits had been left on the wall, a little bit of splendour in all the squalor. I decided they had not made the perilous journey. The pictures had been brought to watch over their children in their new world. I saw them in Sicily, for some reason, dressing up in their hard-earned finery for the photographer. I hoped they never knew the conditions their children came to.

It made me think of my mother's stories about her grandmother bringing up twelve children in a two-bedroom farmhouse in Mid-Wales. We got fed up of these stories as kids. 'So what?' we used to think. She might as well have been talking about The Old Woman Who Lived In A Shoe. It's only as you get older you get to thinking about your own back story, back and back. I thought about Greta too for some reason, about her arrival in America, about her back story. Somehow I couldn't imagine her in such conditions. But before the war many Jews did come from Europe with little more than a suitcase. I decided to ask Greta about it, but it wouldn't be easy. She could clam up if you asked her direct questions. You had to wait for her to offer little bits of information. She didn't give much away about her early life. It was almost as if she were hiding something.

Ewa's own apartment was a studio on W14th Street. It was lined, not so much with the thick sociological tomes I'd imagined, but with a colour-coded audio library of cassettes telling people's stories of Old New York, a little like that of the girl on the tin trunk, I imagined. The first time I went there I wanted to listen to some of them, but Ewa seemed unwilling to share them. Maybe she thought she didn't know me well enough yet. She could be funny like that.

She changed the subject abruptly.

'Is it true that the British say 'fanny' for vagina?' she asked.

'Well, yes,' I said, a little taken aback, and was also surprised when I felt myself blush.

'You know here it's just a cute way of saying ass. When we were about sixteen a friend of mine went over to England to stay with her pen friend. When the family picked her up at the airport, they naturally asked how her flight was. "Fine," she said. "But boy, is my fanny sore." She said their jaws hit the floor, and it took her ages to work out why.'

Truth to tell, I found this evasiveness rather irritating, considering that her work consisted of digging into other people's lives. It was as if she had no-go areas and it could be quite confusing. But most of the time, her sense of fun and easy going nature meant that it was great to be with her. This new part of my life was, of course, in stark contrast to the milieu of the New Cavendish. The next Friday Greta was in a particularly shrewish mood.

'I went to the IRS today,' she informed me accusingly.

'Oh, yes?' I said, putting the trays in order on the table ready for our next opponents.

'I pay more in taxes than you'll earn all year,' she spat, jabbing her finger at me as she did when she wanted to emphasise that she had one over on me. By then I'd got used to her.

'Well, who's that worse for - you or me?'

Greta had no answer and East and West sat down. We played exceptionally well that night, understanding each other perfectly, making barely a mistake, bidding and making the right contracts. We even had a couple of slams – making all thirteen tricks, going through the Blackwood convention flawlessly. Blackwood (named after its inventor no doubt - most conventions are) is one of the most common conventions for finding out if the partnership has enough top cards to bid for slam. Once you've decided you have enough points between you for a slam bid (at least 33), and have decided on your suit, you bid 4NT, which means, 'How many aces do you have partner?' The reply is 5C if you have one or all of the aces, 5D for one, 5H for two and 5S for three. Then if you're happy with the reply, you can bid 5NT, asking for kings. The next reply will inevitably be on the six level, which means you're already into a small slam. You then have to decide if you want to move to the seven level for Grand Slam, and go back into your suit.

Greta perked up no end as we progressed and remained unruffled even at the arrival at the table of her arch-enemy Lily. Lily was full of the Monet exhibition she'd seen at the Metropolitan. She bubbled over with enthusiasm, describing a number of pictures very well.

But Lily was never one for keeping up this kind of cultured talk for very long. Maybe she suddenly caught herself sounding just a little bit pretentious.

'Mind you, one more friggin' water lily and I'd have screamed,' she concluded.

Normally this kind of talk would have drawn a sharp rebuke from Greta. I glanced across and found her lips creased in a girlish pucker, revelling in the joys of doing so well, blithely unaware of what Lily or anyone else was saying. When the evening was over Greta was fairly bristling with anticipation as we waited for Clarke to produce the scores.

She was even more peremptory in this mood than in a bad one, indicating the precise position I was to take up in front of the notice board. When I saw the score I walked slowly back to Greta and mouthed 'Top' at her.

'Top,' she repeated, clasping her hands in some kind of rhapsody, 'top,' and stood up and shook my hand.

When I got back to my apartment Ewa was waiting for me as arranged. She looked stunning in a hugging black and white striped T shirt, cherry red lipstick and pointy fifties-style sunglasses. She was in a fun mood, and had brought a video over for us to watch. It was one of the old black and white films the she loved: Edward G Robinson in *The Red House*. When we started watching it with beer and popcorn, I began to realise it was building up to an image that had haunted me since childhood. It was of someone driving a car into a spooky outhouse that was full of water, and slowly the car sank with the driver at the wheel. But I never knew why. In the film, the building is an old ice-house belonging to the derelict and mysterious Red House in the middle of the woods. Edward G has been exposed as a murderer who killed the woman he loved and the husband who came between them. He gets into his old jalopy, smashes through the ice-house doors and sits patiently waiting for the car to sink. It unsettled me, and I thought it would have been better had it stayed as a vague memory. I asked Ewa why she liked it.

'Oh, I don't know,' she said. 'The mystery, I guess.'

So far, by some instinct I could not name, I'd kept these two worlds apart as much as I could. I'd told Ewa that I played Bridge at a club on

Fridays and left it at that, and had not mentioned Ewa to Greta at all.

She was introduced to Greta in a manner of speaking the next morning. We'd had a lie in. Ewa got up first and woke me with that smell of coffee that always seems much more inviting in America.

'Al', she called, 'Al, come listen to this'.

There was a message on the phone which she played back.

'Hello? Al? I just wanted to say I was so stimulated after last night that I could hardly sleep. Thank you so very much. I hope we can go on playing together for a long, long time.' Click. No name. It was the young, girlish Greta.

We looked at each other and laughed, Ewa a little more reservedly than me, and with a question mark.

'Oh, that's Greta, my Bridge partner. We came top last night.'

'Did we, now? Well, Bridge certainly seems to be a passionate game.' She was still smiling, but there was an edge to her voice.

'Oh, come on. She's seventy-seven if she's a day.'

Ewa laughed again, this time a bit more freely. She bounced into the kitchenette and put on the coffee. It was the first time either of us had got anywhere near proprietary behaviour. How could we make demands on each other when we both wanted to enjoy this relationship, I wondered, without encroaching on each other's lives too much? Ewa didn't seem to want to get too near, sometimes seemed to withdraw a little when she thought she had. Maybe she'd been hurt just one time too many or maybe that was too glib a way of trying to understand her. I was slowly coming out of my shell and my feelings for her were growing. Moments like this gave me cause for hope that hers were for me, but I was afraid that I'd scare her off by moving too close. So the delicate movements of our minuet were a little bewildering. Complicated things, relationships.

Talking of which, I'd had a little spat with Vanessa at work, just when I thought we were getting on so well. We were comfortable together, and frequently told each other to fuck off in a good-natured way. She liked hearing about Wales, although I have to say her notions were a little stereotyped (gleaned from *How Green Was My Valley* no doubt). She told me that some uncles or aunts or whatever had gone to find their roots near Snowdonia somewhere - she couldn't pronounce the name - and were surprised that people were driving around in Mercedes rather than the horses and carts they expected. Neither picture rang true.

On one of the modules, Writing Skills, we sometimes merged our classes and taught together which we both enjoyed. We both had a love of the technicalities of the art, but sometimes used to argue like hell in class, over things like the Oxford Comma, of which she was a fan, but I was not. The students seemed to like this, and Vanessa pointed out that it gave them differing points of view and developed their confidence.

For one of their assignments they had to submit a portfolio of ten pieces of writing in different styles - a review, a sports report, a travel piece and so on. I set about marking them and then passed twenty per cent of them on to her for 'second marking' as I did with hers. She came storming into my office, as she was sometimes wont to do, shouting that I hadn't marked them correctly. Each piece should have been given five separate marks for style, accuracy etc, which would mean fifty separate bits of feedback for one assignment. These should have been written in her infamous 'rubrics' which other lecturers, I knew, did their best to dodge. I too thought this ridiculous, and in any case she hadn't discussed any of this with me beforehand. It was one of her downfalls. She was a great teacher and kept across all the latest trends in journalism and pedagogy, but sometimes overlooked details.

I don't respond well to people shouting at me and gave as good as I got, saying something like there should be a proper system that everyone understood, like there was in Cardiff.

This stopped her in her tracks. Her eyes narrowed and her mouth dropped into almost a snarl.

'Do you realise how patronising that sounds?'

'Oh, Vanessa, no-one's trying to patronise you. You should have told me how you wanted this marked in the first place, not barge in here a day before deadline ranting and raving.'

In the end she begrudgingly allowed me to stick to my original style of feedback, but I was angry at the way she reacted when she was in the wrong.

The evening after there were some leaving drinks for a colleague in the bar across the street. I felt obliged to go and thought I might be able to avoid Vanessa, but she collared me when I was getting some drinks.

'I'm sorry. I was such a jerk yesterday,' she said.

Maybe she wanted me to wave it away and tell her she was not a jerk. My impulse was to agree with her, but I settled for smiling coolly and going back to join my crowd.

The next Friday Greta was a little frosty at first, back to her old self. Did she want to put me back in my place, or was she punishing herself for her rather gushing phone message? I couldn't quite see that. Neither of us referred to it. But at the end of the evening - we managed only second this time - she invited me round to supper a week on Saturday.

'Nothing too fancy,' she said, with a deprecating little wave of her hand which fooled nobody. For a full minute I wondered if it was just coincidence that she issued her invitation when Lily was sitting at the table. But then of course I saw that it could not be. Lily in Greta's eyes was far from the right side of town. She would take her revenge by making exclusive uptown social arrangements under her nose.

'It'll just be you, Sandra and Pamela, if you won't find the company of three old women too tiresome'.

Lily put her finger in her mouth as if she were about to vomit.

Sandra was the nearest thing Greta had to a friend, as far as I could see: a fluffy, white-haired old lady invariably introduced with the phrase 'and her daughter's a concert pianist.' Sandra once added to me sotto voce, 'My daughter teaches music in the public system and plays the piano in school concerts'. Pamela was another Upper East Side matron, even more snobbish than Greta. Although, that's not quite right. For all her faults and rudeness, I didn't have any evidence to suggest that Greta was a snob. She treated everyone with equal contempt.

'I'll look forward to it', I said, almost sincerely. I heard Lily give a little snort.

The next afternoon I was walking round the Shakespeare Garden in Central Park with Ewa. She introduced me to it - a shrubbery on a bank where they grow every plant and flower mentioned in the plays.

'It's my birthday next Saturday,' she said as we admired the myrtle. 'I thought we could go out to Coney Island in the afternoon and then back to my parents place for dinner. It's kind of tradition'.

I could tell immediately what a big deal this was. She'd never even mentioned her family before. And I made the mistake of not saying anything, but leaning forward and kissing her.

Chapter Seven

It was a mistake because it put me immediately into an impossible situation. Why didn't I just say: 'I'm sorry, I'd love to, but I've got something else on I just can't get out of'? Well, I guess I know why. What I wanted to do was to meet Ewa's family, to work on our budding but hesitant relationship, to see if it would blossom. Because increasingly I felt that's what I wanted it to do.

But how could I let down Greta, and with what consequences? I depended on our Bridge together now, like a drug, to see me from one week to the next. I could see her now, girlishly, excitedly, but meticulously planning her 'nothing fancy' supper. It would occupy her entire week.

I would have to do something, I knew, but couldn't for the life of me figure out what. So of course I did nothing.

I was still dithering the next Tuesday, when I went to the New Cav and played with Marco. I was still trying to make him out too. He was a hard guy to read or talk to. He didn't seem to want anything from anybody. Even though his bidding was practiced enough, it sometimes went off into realms I couldn't reach. I didn't know then whether these flights were pure brilliance, loss of concentration, ineptitude or a heady brew of all of the above. In my mind I made up a story about him that he was the brilliant but rebellious son of a well-to-do Long Island family, forced by his manicured mother to endure long evenings of Bridge as a teenager, vowing to his seething inward self to beat her at her own game and reject all her values into the bargain.

As I've pointed out, Marco was never one to waste words but he seemed silently to blame me, with a glare, when things went wrong. I enjoyed playing with him, but unlike with Greta and me, we struggled to find that easy exchange of information in the bidding. Bid Bold, Play Safe, was one of the maxims I'd picked up. But Marco and I kind of reversed it, because we were never sure of each other in the bidding. Bid safe, play bold. A recipe for disaster.

Anyway, this one evening Marco and I were doing OK, our cautious bidding paying off for once. I noticed Sandra playing South a couple of tables down. Like me she hated scoring so avoided sitting North, but didn't like moving around too much. So South was her ideal position. I'd always had the impression, based on the merest fragments of evidence, that she'd been Greta's regular partner until she could stand it no more. I didn't have the chance to talk to her until the end, when I suddenly thought I could ask her advice about Greta's party. But as soon as I mentioned Greta's name, Sandra said, 'That Sonofabithch! Pardon my French'.

I'm not easily shocked but somehow those words coming out of the mouth of this American Miss Marple took me aback. It turned out that Sandra's daughter - the alleged concert pianist - wanted to bring the grandchildren over that Saturday while she and her husband went on one of their very rare nights out. Sandra wasn't going to pass up this longed-for chance to grandmother the kids so before coming out that night had called Greta to cry off.

'You should have heard what she said to me. It was as if I'd gone out of my way to sabotage her Goddam party. Really, you must excuse my language. I'm not normally such a potty-mouth but she drives me to it. She's impossible. I really can't think why you put up with her.'

For mild-mannered Sandra to launch into this full-scale campaign must have taken quite an earful from Greta, outrageous even to the both of us who knew her so well.

'Anyway, she said she'd have to call the whole thing off and slammed down the phone'.

I could have hugged Sandra there and then, of course, but made do with a friendly grasp of the shoulder, disguised as sympathy.

On the subway home I refined my strategy. I'd call Greta tomorrow to confirm and stoically receive the sad news of the cancellation. But when I finally succeeded in undoing the three locks of my apartment door the phone was ringing.

'I've had to postpone Saturday evening,' - Greta never announced herself on the phone - 'because Sandra has let me down. I think it's most discourteous.' I hadn't uttered a word yet. 'You put yourself out for people, welcome them into your home, and this is how they repay you. It'll have to be the Saturday after. I trust you can make it'.

'Ah, ye-es, I'm pretty sure I can, let me see,' I said, thumbing through the phone book for sound effects. 'Yes, that should be fine.'

'Good. I hope this hasn't put you out.'

I could barely disguise my glee. 'No, Greta, it hasn't put me out.'

'See you Friday. Call to confirm first.'

At the club on Friday I noticed that Greta and Sandra didn't even acknowledge each other. As we were sitting there waiting for East and West, Greta started to launch into more invective against her closest friend. I forestalled her.

'So will Sandra be coming a week tomorrow?'

'Oh, yes. Never fear. Now that she's got everyone to arrange things to suit her.'

'Greta, you shouldn't be too hard on her,' I said, in a feeble attempt to defend Sandra.

'I'm just being honest,' said Greta. This was her stock response whenever I tried to pull her up on her rude remarks.

At this point East and West shuffled up. They were an elderly couple who spent the entire time between games arguing about who should have bid, led or played what in the previous game. They were still at it now as they sat down, and all the other tables had started playing. Greta looked disgusted at this behaviour.

'How gracious of you to join us,' she snapped, glowering at each in turn. 'Do you think we're sitting here for our own amusement?'

The disagreeable couple did the usual routine of staring at Greta, at each other, and then at me as if for explanation.

'Let's get on with the game,' I said lamely, taking my hand from the compartment in the metal tray in the centre of the table.

We didn't play so well that night, both a bit cross with the other. We missed a small slam - that's all but one of the tricks - and it costs us hundreds of points. Greta had opened 2C, one of the strongest opening bids you can make, promising 23 points or more. I'd replied two in my strongest suit, diamonds. I had ten points so we would have had enough for slam. But this was a standard weak reply, so Greta stopped at 3NT, whereas we should have been in 6NT. An egregious mistake.

I expected a mouthful from Greta afterwards. But in one of her unpredictable yet characteristic changes of mood, she became quite the mentor. This was one of the intriguing aspects of her personality. Just when you thought of a word to fit her like a glove, she'd do something to contradict it completely.

'You know, after a 2C opening we should play Steps. It gives you a precise point count, and you know exactly where you are: a reply of 2D means you have 0-4 points, 2H means 5-7, 2S 8-10 and 2NT means more than 10. You should have replied 2S'.

She enjoyed giving me these little lessons, being able to teach me things. And I was grateful for it. But I wished she wouldn't make such a meal of it.

The next morning revealed a clear, crisp November day and I was looking forward to the trip out to Coney Island and Ewa's parents' house near Prospect Park. Yes, looking forward…..It was the first time I could remember in ages that I got out of bed with a little leap instead of my customary crawl. I'd never been to Brooklyn before. Generally we were still wary about speaking to others at the faculty about any relationship, but I had told a couple of people at work I was going to Brooklyn. There were the usual Manhattanite jibes about jabs and passports.

We met outside the Flatiron building - one of my favourites in the city - and took the F train to Coney Island, which for me had the glamorous undertones gleaned from those old black and white films we watched as kids on rainy Sunday afternoons. For Ewa it naturally held more personal memories, as she told me on the endless journey down on the subway, which for most of the way down to the southern tip of the borough was on elevated tracks so I got a good view. She remembered sunny Sunday afternoons, going down with her father on one of those irreclaimable childhood outings when life lived up to its promises.

As Ewa recounted these tales of small, infinite joys - she was never happier than when telling a story - I could see what the Manhattanites meant by passports. It was a different country down here. Even though I'd got fairly used to the subway by now I was nervous about coming this far out, remembering the film *Death Wish* which gave the very strong impression that you took your life in your hands with every journey.

There was indeed that lurking sense of menace, both inside and outside. Inside the sparsely populated carriage an assortment of characters studiously avoided eye contact except the odd nutter talking to himself, or you, or some other unfathomable voice he could hear or wanted to hear. One brightly dressed middle-aged woman sported a badge saying 'We're a nation of immigrants.' Outside street upon scruffy street of terraced houses (row houses as they call them here) or flats trundled by, punctuated by wired-in sports courts. But I liked it. There was something that attracted me to it, something real. I looked back and could see the Chrysler, Empire State and other towers glinting in the sunshine, like some far-off Oz.

As we got closer to Coney Island, it got even more desolate, dilapidated Brownstones giving way to two-storey houses. The funfair itself was still vast but clearly past its prime, and with a different air of menace behind the seedy glitter. Despite my excitement I couldn't help thinking of Barry Island out of season, the little funfair on a peninsula west of Cardiff, even though Coney Island must be ten times the size. There was something familiar about it.

We went on a couple of rides, eating candy floss and behaving like teenagers. The view from the Ferris wheel over the harbour and back across the Brooklyn flats to the gleaming city was mesmerising and I could hardly tear my eyes away. We strolled along the boardwalk to

Brighton Beach, past Little Odessa full of half empty shops with their Cyrillic signs, groups of men sitting at oil-clothed tables sipping tea or vodka. Ewa delighted in showing me everything. I'd rarely seen her so animated. I found myself hoping that we were entering a new phase in the relationship, at least one where we could admit we were having one.

We took the B Train back up to Prospect Park and walked over to Flatbush Avenue. I felt safe in her hands: this was her home ground and she seemed quite at ease. It was a real eye-opener for me though. Flatbush Avenue was teeming: street stalls here, shoddy stores there, piles of garbage ranging from disemboweled black bags to three-seater sofas everywhere. People seemed relaxed on the surface but there was a watchfulness, a wariness. We were under close surveillance. Young middle class white couples were not all that common here.

I was relieved when we turned off the Avenue into a quiet side street. Here was Ewa's home, an old-fashioned town house with big bay windows revealing wooden shutters inside. Steep steps led to a double front door, with long glass panels starting about six inches from the ground, surrounded by dark wood. It had a prim but hardly prosperous air about it.

I don't know what exactly I'd been expecting, but it wasn't this all American family. Maybe from what Ewa had told me of them, I'd got a vague Hollywood picture of a heavy-accented Polish family swigging vodka and slurping barszcz, as I believe the Polish spelling of bortsch goes. In fact we were offered a glass of krulpnik - vodka and honey - to warm us as we came in. The only other real Polishness in evidence was an exquisite Black Madonna on the wall, no doubt a cherished family heirloom.

The interior had almost a wartime feel to it, more by design than neglect, I thought. We sat at a huge wooden table in the dining room, separated from the living room by sliding mahogany doors, topped by a sort of ornate wooden pelmet. It had a dark paper, figuring large pears and grapes. Through the door I could see the unfitted kitchen and its huge dresser with a marble top.

Ewa's family consisted of her father Greg, her mother Maria, her two older brothers and their families, and a handful of neighbours, clearly a close community. I was pleasantly surprised to find that, although everyone was perfectly friendly and courteous, no-one showed undue curiosity about me. Maybe they were used to Ewa's men friends coming and going. It did mean though I could relax, especially as the beer, wine and vodka started to flow.

We ate pot roast and ice-cream cake. You couldn't get more American fare. The children were having their meal around the kitchen table next door. Storytelling was clearly the traditional entertainment at such dos. Ewa's father had been a docker all his life, or longshoreman as Americans quaintly call them. Long retired, he was full of stories of his work, tragic and comic, big and small. His sons, one a teacher in a local high school and the other something on Wall Street but who also lived locally, egged him on, prompting him to retell the ones they knew by heart but gave a good show of enjoying yet again.

'What about the one when you had a cargo of Irish whisky, Pop? And some of the guys managed to mislay a crate?'

'And that time with the bananas from the Caribbean and all the spiders?'

Ewa in contrast seemed to want him to tell stories of his childhood on the farm in Poland.

'Tell Al about going hunting with your father, Dad,' she said. 'What about the one with the pig?'

Greg seemed reluctant to hark back too much to his pre-American life - his heart wasn't in it and he would quickly return to Brooklyn. And her mother seemed to resent Ewa's attempts to prompt tales of the old country. I got the impression she came from cultured stock, had come to America during the war a few years after Greg. They were both clearly proud of their successful family, and looked to them now, rather than back. But I could see why Ewa had all those tapes of immigrants' stories lining her walls; she was so hungry for the knowledge about her own past, her ancestry, that her family would prefer to forget. The tapes filled the gaps in her life, made up for the things her family wouldn't tell her.

Her quest interrupted the rhythm of the evening. There were tensions around the table. It was as if Ewa couldn't forget her role as social observer and recorder, wanted to memorialise the old culture of a country her parents were glad to have escaped. Perhaps as a woman she felt excluded from these tales of man's work. Perhaps that's a sexist way of looking at things. My heart did go out to her – she seemed so much of an outsider in her own family, dominated by the men. This was their notion of oral history, sitting round the table swigging back the booze telling stories, not recording them, classifying them, analysing them.

At the same time I couldn't help wishing she'd lighten up and enjoy herself. I was annoyed because we usually had such a good time together, but here with her family she seemed like a different person. And it was her family's company I was enjoying.

I tried to ease these with stories of my own. My parents were both teachers, my father from a mining family and my mother from a farming one. The stories went down reasonably well. I also asked questions about life on the farm back in Poland and Greg, momentarily distracted, would drift into some half-remembered tale, only to return with gusto to the early days in Brooklyn when each penny counted.

I thought I noticed Maria give me a gratified, grateful smile. Ewa, on the other hand, seemed put out, as if I'd hijacked the conversation, but the evening did recapture some of its earlier jocularity. It passed quickly and I found, a little to my surprise and Ewa's annoyance, that I'd had a great time.

As we were leaving, and coats were being found and donned, Maria grasped me by the hand and said in rather a low voice, 'We so much enjoyed having you. I hope you'll come again. We never know with Ewa's friends'.

She tried to make light of the remark with a little laugh, but I detected behind it some real concern - or was it hurt?

It was only in the cab on the way back into the city that Ewa started to wind down a little. I wondered about her awkwardness with her family, but judged it wise not to probe. It made me think about my own family's stories, happily trotted out when we were young and uninterested, but difficult for them to conjure up to order. I made my mind up to try to find more about my own background when I went back for Christmas. It also struck me how difficult Ewa's work was, to find people who would reel off childhood tales. It occurred to me that she may feel guilty about leaving that world behind for academia across the water in Manhattan, just a few miles away but a different world altogether. This was so different from Dad's background in the Rhondda, say, where getting an education and escaping the pits was something prized by all concerned. As the lights of the Battery Tunnel strobed the cab with oddly eerie, melodramatic flashes of light, I reflected she may not be aware of her guilt, or may have buried it somewhere.

'What are you thinking?' she asked suddenly, snuggling up to me a little.

'Oh, just how pleasant it was,' I answered, looking out of the window at the tiles whizzing past in a blur.

'Hmm, for you maybe.'

'Not for you, then?'

'Well, I just find them so....so incurious about their culture and history. It drives me crazy.'

'Perhaps you're judging them by your own work. Isn't it their own way of doing the same thing? I thought they were nice and natural.'

'Mmm, if your benchmark is the Adams Family. It's all very well for Dad to play at Happy Families, but the truth is he's been cheating on Mom for years. Just can't keep his dick inside his pants.'

'Does your mother know?'

'She probably suspects. We've never acknowledged it. But everyone else knows.'

'How do you know?'

'Common knowledge in the neighbourhood.'

'One woman?'

'If only.'

Frosty Ewa had returned. I never knew when she would. She shifted away from me on the seat and stared studiously out of the window. There it was again, this strange, inside-out tango - move close to your partner, move away again. This did help explain a few things - her fear of commitment for one. But then, it was a fear I shared.

'At least they didn't show too much curiosity about your escort'. I smiled across at her, but she didn't smile back. And then I thought: maybe they've learnt not to.

Chapter Eight

At Bridge the next Friday, Greta was a little cold at first, almost arch. It was as if she knew I'd been up to something, running around with someone else. When she'd asked me, in one of our first conversations, if I was married, I'd said yes, for some reason. Simplicity I suppose, and the avoidance of further explanation. I'd told her that Megan couldn't leave her job so we had to be apart for the time being. But now I couldn't undo it and when Greta regularly asked after her I felt obliged to give a little more than, 'She's fine, thank you', after the first couple of times. So it was, 'She's had a cold but she's getting over it', or, 'She's just been on a shopping trip to London with a friend.'

Of course I hadn't heard a breath from Megan for several months now, and each time Greta asked after her was something of an ordeal. I could not, naturally, mention anything about Ewa, but had the feeling that Greta suspected something.

Greta soon thawed out though, as a kittenish excitement about her dinner party the next day won through. To my utter surprise, she informed me she'd invited Marco. The only time she ever acknowledged him was when I mentioned him, and then she'd never fail to find a way of putting him down.

'He always seems…..unwashed,' she'd said one evening, choosing her word. She was a lady, after all.

'He's from a very good family,' I said, having no clue about his background. But I knew this was a winner with Greta. At least it shut her up, and must have swung the invitation.

He'd become my regular partner now on Tuesdays, and didn't come very often on Fridays. I'd taken to him, although resented him slightly because he was one of those guys who was completely disheveled and unkempt but somehow managed to be the most dashing man in the room. His hair windswept and unwashed, the neglect of a stubble round his chin, his holey tweed jacket a couple of sizes too big for him, he was effortlessly debonair. When I looked like that, people asked me if I was alright.

He was sociable enough but didn't socialise, at least not with us. He flouted the very conventions I was struggling to learn. At Bridge clubs you don't pitch your cards in the middle of the table, you place them in an ordered row in front of you. That way you can always discuss the hands afterwards, or investigate who played what in the event of a challenge. So everyone sits straight and square to the table, except Marco, of course. He slouched in his chair, his crossed leg dangling over the side, and virtually flung his cards onto to the green baize in the manner of a movie cowboy throwing cards into a hat.

This was very bad form, but oddly Marco went unchallenged, even by Greta on the rare occasion that he did turn up on a Friday. The one surprising thing they did have in common was a profound love of the New York Yankees. They'd been in the play-offs of the World Series that year and so they could discuss play and form. Clearly I was useless to Greta for this purpose. Even though I had had the rules explained to me several times and had even gone with Ewa to see them play, the language of the game kept it by and large a mystery for me. It was one of the few times that Greta seemed human to me, when she was discussing baseball. The rest of the time she took no notice of Marco whatsoever, her lips just a little more pursed than usual.

So I couldn't quite figure out why she wanted him over to dinner, let alone why he'd accepted. Maybe she'd decided that all the Bridge ladies and me wouldn't make for a very balanced evening. Or did she have a little soft spot for the dashing Marco, for all her straight-laced exterior?

'Be there at seven sharp,' she said as we were leaving. 'I don't hold with tardiness.'

Once the difficulties of the date had been sorted out, I thought I'd make a bit of an effort for her party. I had my only suit cleaned and pressed, and even bought a tie. I got there about ten minutes before the appointed hour, so nervous was I to do things right. It was one of those old-fashioned apartment blocks on swanky Central Park East, a green awning over the front door opening into a spacious lobby with a marble fireplace, huge gilt-framed mirrors and sprawling, chunky sofas.

The doorman rang up to announce me and directed me up to the tenth floor in one of those old elevators with a sliding metal trellis gate. It opened into a wide corridor and Greta's door was opposite. I pressed the buzzer, wondering what the evening held in store. She opened it herself, threw up her hands and said, 'My, you look a proper mensch.'

I wasn't sure what the word meant but determined to take it as a compliment. (I looked it up in the dictionary later and it said, 'Honest, decent person.' If only she knew.).

'Here, let me look at you,' and she proffered her cheek for a peck. She was playing the part of the hostess to a tee.

The ladies were already there - clearly as terrified of being late as I'd been - sitting primly sipping glasses of sherry. I was offered a Bourbon and took it. Greta evidently had fixed ideas of what ladies and mensches should drink. Marco was clearly, predictably late.

'Excuse me ladies, while I give Al here the tour'.

The apartment was stunning, immaculate - straight off the cover of a glossy magazine. There were large sliding patio doors leading out to a little terrace, with fantastic views over Central Park. Greta pointed out landmarks here and there. I leant over the rail and saw the Empire State Building way down to the left. The interior was no less impressive, carpeted throughout in plush cream, with linen coloured drapes and sofas. There was lots of pewter, silver and glass. The centrepiece was a stained-glass window mounted on the wall and backlit.

'That's Venetian glass', she said, with the wave of a hand and the air of a chatelaine showing someone round the west wing. The dining area was the foot of an L, with a large polished table, elegantly set, and a huge sideboard with more silver on it.

'That's from the Old Country.' She used this phrase once in a while, but never elaborated on it. Again I had a vision of her growing up in Vienna before the war, in a large house with servants, then fleeing the Nazis with her family. I was still not quite sure where the Old Country was, and remembered the promise I made to myself in the old tenement building in the Lower East Side to ask her. But would I have the courage?

The other side of the main room was a carved card table with four high rattan-backed chairs.

'Maybe we can have a few hands later on'. She could probably see me counting up the guests. One too many for a foursome.

'You others can go ahead - I won't mind, ' said Greta the Martyr. This was a new one. I couldn't buy it somehow.

The inventory went on and on; this silk print from Singapore, those chairs from Rome. Items were described in terms of the provenance - Greta clearly enjoyed the memories of her trips with her husband. It turned out they'd built up a chain of furniture stores together - from scratch, I was given to understand.

At last the tour was over and we joined the others, to be regaled with many stories of her legendary entertaining. 'Oh, yes, I was quite a party girl.' This was so incongruous that at first I thought she said 'patty' - an American word for a kind of pasty. This was how a Bostonian would pronounce party. But then the image of Greta stuffing her face with thick-crust Cornish pasties was equally as ridiculous. I exchanged glances with the others and she must have mistaken our smiles for admiration, as if to say: 'What a woman.'

So, encouraged as she thought she was, she embarked on a long log of lavish and successful parties for eminent personages.

'I keep Kosher, you know,' she said as a preamble to an evening featuring a well-known Argentine Jew, as if this made her culinary achievements all the more remarkable. 'He said to me afterwards it was the most delicious meal he'd ever tasted.'

'How nice,' we simpered.

Marco was of course very late. It was with some relief that I finally heard a loud impatient rap on the door.

'Doesn't he know what doorbells are for?' muttered Greta as she went to answer it. 'Well, it wouldn't surprise me.'

As she opened it, Marco was slumped against the doorjamb, a half-smoked cigarette drooping from his lips, as scruffy and unshaven as ever, not a hair in place. Now I saw him there, I was surprised that he'd turned up at all.

He shuffled in and nodded at us. Greta gave him a disapproving look as she thrust a cut-glass ashtray in front of him and a Bourbon into his hand, but didn't say anything about his unpunctuality. Gentlemen's vices were clearly to be tolerated by the perfect hostess. Marco was oblivious. He plonked himself down in an elegant Italian chair and there was a sharp crack. Everyone looked at Greta for her reaction. She merely gave a shrug as if to say, 'Well, what do you expect?' and we all rushed to inspect the damage. Marco looked annoyed as if he considered he'd been given inferior seating. I was amazed that Greta took it all so lightly. She certainly threw herself into the hostess role with the utmost aplomb. There was a large splinter in the leg of the chair.

'Can it be fixed?' I enquired of Greta. She was staring at it, but not examining it closely as I was doing.

'I expect so,' she said resignedly, as if the evening was already living down to her expectations.

'You'll have to send me the bill,' mumbled Marco.

'Oh, I surely will. Maybe now is a good time to eat,' she said, ushering us towards the dining room with a stately sweep of her arm.

You had to hand it to the old girl - she knew how to put on a spread: chicken soup, Waldorf salad, a beautiful salmon brought whole to the table which she asked me to serve, accompanied by Meursault, profiteroles with Vouvray, excellent French cheeses with Graves, sliced apple and celery and a huge bowl of walnuts. Everything from soup to nuts, as Greta herself would say, was cookery-book perfect. The same went for the table: white china edged with blue and gold, doily-like blue lace placemats, blue linen napkins in silver rings, cut glass and pear-shaped decanters.

How very like Greta, herself always immaculately turned out, never a hair out of place as they say. I recalled a discussion I'd had with her at the club, one of those odd debates we got into while waiting for the next couple. She must have passed a remark on someone who didn't come up to her standards of presentation, no doubt within their hearing, and pronounced it cost nothing to be well groomed, seemingly unaware of the absurdity of her remark. I begged to differ, saying many people around the world could not afford food, let alone hair-dos. She ignored this, as she usually did responses which flatly contradicted her, or were alien to her own world. I pressed on, saying that anyway people were more interesting if they looked lived-in, rather than out of the pages of a catalogue. Like houses. A house you walked into for the first time was far more intriguing if there were an open book lying on the sofa, a coffee table stained with candle wax and wine, a pile of jazz CDs scattered on the floor. Greta had rejoined the debate with renewed vigour. This was nonsense, and I should smarten myself up while I was at it. I recalled her words now, and how I was strangely hurt, thinking she never took Marco up on his appearance.

It was a tense meal. Everyone concentrated hard on replacing the wine bottle on the silver coaster without spilling any, and on eating as quietly as possible, with the result that knives seemed to hit china with the roar of jackhammers on tarmac. Greta maintained an elegant calm throughout, disregarding Marco's wisecracks. She somewhat dominated the conversation, with yet more tales of dinners, voyages, business successes. Our own feeble attempts to reciprocate were largely quashed.

Marco at one awful point got fed up with this, cut across one of Greta's endless yarns and asked me, 'So how's the new little girlfriend shaping up?'

Christ. I'd confided to him about Ewa one night over a drink after Bridge, never thinking for a moment he'd have the chance of bringing it up in front of Greta. She clunked her glass on the table and I could feel her sharp look like a physical blow. I was conscious of the blush rising up my face and I no longer remember what I blurted out. Nothing more was said, but I had the strongest feeling that something would be the next Friday. I don't know if I imagined it, but I thought the atmosphere got even frostier after this.

Conversation, as strained as it was, turned towards accents, and the oddly enduring American fascination with the English one. The others asked me for some Britishisms, as they termed it, and the difference between the Welsh accent and the English. Despite my best efforts, I couldn't get them to distinguish between them.

'My mother was British,' Greta announced all of a sudden.

'Your mother was British?' I repeated, not managing to keep a note of incredulity out of my voice. Why had she not mentioned this before? 'Where was she from?' I asked.

'Oh I can't remember. But we always used to have tea on the stroke of four. That's British, isn't it?'

'And what was your father?'

'Austrian of course. We grew up in Vienna.'

So I'd been right about Vienna. But she'd never once before spoken of her mother. Most Americans I'd met were fascinated with their ethnicity. It didn't ring true somehow. I'd noticed that her accent wasn't what I thought of as typically American, but it wasn't British either. More like those clipped tones women had in the old films from the 1930s. Surely she would have known phrases like 'the bee's knees' if she had a British mother? But why would Greta lie about it? It couldn't be attention seeking, could it? I was eager for more information.

'Was she Jewish too?'

'Of course,' said Greta, now looking as if the whole subject had begun to bore her. I remembered too late that Judaism passed through the maternal line, so it was a particularly stupid question. But I pressed on.

'So is that why you came to America? Because you were Jews? What happened to your parents?'

I knew as soon as I'd uttered the words I'd overstepped the mark, been crass. Greta kept her cards close to her chest in more ways than one. Sandra and Pamela exchanged embarrassed glances and started to fidget.

'Shall we go next door for coffee?' said Greta, getting up from the table to fetch it from the kitchen.

'Why? We don't even know them,' cracked Marco. I couldn't help give a little chuckle, while Pamela and Sandra giggled like schoolchildren misbehaving when Teacher's back was turned.

Pamela got up and followed Greta. 'Here, let me help you.'

'No. Go sit down. I can manage.'

'I insist.'

'I tell you, no. I prefer to do it myself.'

But Pamela, well-versed in the social niceties. was trying to wrest the coffee jug from her. As she did a large slop splashed onto the cream carpet.

'There. I knew that would happen,' said Greta, a glint of something close to triumph in her eye. 'Didn't I warn you?'

'Oh,' was all Pamela could say, her hand covering her mouth.

'I think you'd all better go,' announced Greta. We all looked at her to see if she meant it. 'I'll get your coats.' She clearly did.

'But don't lets spoil a perfect evening,' ventured Sandra. 'Look, we can soon clean it up. Baking soda is good for coffee.'

Greta was already on her way to the cloakroom. 'Just go, Sandra,' she boomed, and came back with our coats. We were bundled out of the door unceremoniously like those naughty schoolchildren. She virtually slammed it behind us.

'Well!' said Pamela, recovering her dignity.

'Come on, we're well out of it,' said Sandra, taking her by the arm.

'How about a beer?' said Marco, looking at me.

'I can't make the old bat out,' I said to Marco as we sank a couple in a nearby bar.

'I don't know why you even bother,' drawled Marco, looking around us in his usual distracted way.

'There's something about her that intrigues me,' I mused, as much to myself as to him, I suppose. 'It's as if I keep expecting to find a redeeming quality in her.'

'And the best of British luck to you, buddy. Why do you worry about her – seriously?'

'Well, I suppose I do think there's some good in all of us, that we're here for a reason.'

'You really believe that?'

'No, I guess it's just nice to believe in it sometimes. Like fate. It's easier to believe that things are mapped out, have a point, make some kind of sense at least, even if we can't see it. Know what I mean?'

'Yeah, at times, I guess,' he said, crumpling up his mouth and wiggling his head from side to side as he weighed up his answer. 'But it's just clutching at straws – nothing to do with reality. Of course there's no master plan, no sense to be made of. Who would come up with a plan like this?' He threw both hands up in the air, and I could tell he meant life in general, rather than New York City, which he loved.

'You old cynic. I'll find out something good about her, you wait and see. And when I do you'll be the first to know.'

'Care to make it interesting?' he asked, rubbing his thumb and forefinger together as Greta had done that last time I saw her.

'Why not?' I said.

We settled on a stake of a hundred bucks. Before we shook on it though we had a discussion about the criteria for deeming something a redeeming feature. Something that had benefitted humanity? Too general. A random act of kindness? Too specific. In the end we compromised and agreed it should be something that had changed someone's life for the better. I felt quite buoyed by the fact that I now had a mission: to find One Good Thing about Greta.

'I dropped a real clanger, didn't I, with that question about her parents?'

'Why? It's normal here. She was the one who brought up the subject of her mother. And anyway, she's hardly Miss Manners herself, is she?'

'I'm not convinced about her British mother,' I said. 'Why does she hate the world?'

'Oh, fuck her. She's such a snob. If I were you I'd concentrate on that girlfriend of yours.'

'And another thing. Greta thinks I'm still happily married. So please don't mention Ewa to her again.'

Marco pulled a face as if to say there was something weird going on which he didn't understand and didn't want to. He didn't show any curiosity about what I'd just said. There was a time, not so long ago, when I'd have welcomed this lack of inquisitiveness about my relationships, but now I wanted to open up to him. I must be getting better.

So instead I turned the tables on him and asked how he got into the

Bridge habit. I'd been trying to picture a young Marco in a swish room learning the intricacies of the game while his mates were outside shooting hoops. I'd failed. It turned out his mother had died in childbirth and he was brought up by an aunt. Bridge was the one way he had of keeping close to his father, who was mad about it and loved teaching his son. Marco related all this in his matter-of-fact, almost bored way. It explained things I hadn't been able to figure out about him - the lone-wolf, the outsider, the emotional detachment. We made a night of it, and things began to blur towards the end. But I came away thinking that I'd made my first real friend in New York. Couldn't count Greta, and Ewa was becoming more of an enigma the closer I got to her. The feminine mystique was more of a puzzle to me than ever.

I'd been thinking about Ewa quite a bit in the last week. I was still unsure about what to make of our relationship. We enjoyed each other, but there was something in the partnership that wasn't working. We couldn't seem to play as a team. I couldn't help contrasting this with the understanding Greta and I had as Bridge partners - although I tried hard not to. Maybe there was someone between us. Maybe she too had been hurt enough in the past to value her independence above all else. Maybe deep down she mistrusted men, even resented them. Lots of maybes, no definites.

Since we'd gone to her parents' place she'd been quite cool. She'd come round to my apartment one evening in the week and brought some Chinese food to go, out of those little cartons just like in the movies. We'd shared a couple of bottles of wine, rather unequally in my favour it must be said, and I thought we were having quite a good time. Then at eleven o'clock she suddenly got up and announced she should be getting back. This had happened a couple of times before but I thought we were moving on somewhere. My first instinct was to try to persuade her to stay, but my second was not to, and I didn't.

The day after Greta's dinner party was a cold, sunny Sunday. I'd got to enjoy my Sunday mornings, drinking coffee in my leather chair and listening to National Public Radio on WNYC. I rang Ewa late in the morning to see if she fancied brunch.

'What are you up to?'

'A late breakfast and the papers,' she said, munching away. Plan A was out then.

'Fancy doing anything this afternoon?' I asked, trying to match her cool and at the same time reflecting this would get us nowhere. In the end she suggested we get a train up the Hudson to Hyde Park, the family home of Franklin D Roosevelt. Eleanor was a particular heroine of hers.

I met her at the information booth at Grand Central. I still got a thrill every time I went inside the station, so grand and central was it. I'd decided it was the most beautiful interior in New York. The train ride right alongside the majestic Hudson was equally as exhilarating, and amazing to think that the mayhem of Manhattan was just a few miles away.

I was entranced by Hyde Park in its every detail: the musty library where I could almost hear those scratchy wartime phone calls across the Atlantic to Churchill in his own country home at Chartwell; the convertible in the garage with its special mechanism for delivering cigarettes to the polio-stricken President. I tried describing Churchill's equally atmospheric home. But Ewa was more interested in the bedroom of Mrs R senior, separating those of her son and daughter-in-law, and the little house in the woods where in later years Eleanor spent more and more of her time with her female companion. She must have caught me focusing on something else when she was telling me about Eleanor, and immediately got the hump. She always seemed to want to be in control, and got upset when I did anything to challenge it, as she saw it, such as look away when she was telling me something interesting. And with one of the horrible flashes of insight that strike you sometimes, I thought this was how I must have been with Megan. There I was thinking that our marriage was so democratic, when all the time I believed deep down, without being aware of it, that what was good for me was good for her.

The sun was setting spectacularly as the train sped back along the river towards the city, and even the Tappen Zee Bridge and Yonkers looked romantic. It should have been a perfect afternoon, but somehow we just weren't clicking. A couple of times I steeled myself to say something, to try to talk about how or where things were going, but I couldn't bring myself to. I realised I was still a little cross with her for pooping the party at her parents' place. And while she was usually at her best showing me around, giving snippets of history about a place and its people, she too seemed buttoned up and grumpy.

As we pulled into Grand Central I was still deliberating whether to ask her for a drink or dinner. I wondered if she were wondering the same thing. But she pre-empted me, saying she had some work to finish for tomorrow. We pecked each other on the cheek, smiled awkwardly and promised to call.

The week went by and neither of us did. And a couple of times I'd made up my mind to call it a day with Greta. Her performance at the dinner party was beyond the pale, even for her. I no longer wanted to be her accomplice in her vindictive campaigns. And some part of me even wondered if it was she who was coming between me and Ewa. Could she possibly resent my sacred Fridays? She did sometimes suggest doing something, but I always found an excuse. Surely she couldn't be jealous of

Greta? She did ask questions about her. And when she heard my descriptions she would wonder aloud, like Marco, why I kept up the partnership. I wondered too. Maybe I should be more active in my quest for Greta's One Good Thing. And if I ditched Greta, it would mean turning my back on the New Cavendish too. I could always look for another club, I supposed, but it was one of the best in town and now I felt at home there. It anchored me in my Meganless sea.

So come Friday, I rang Greta, looking forward to some light relief at the end of a gloomy week, But she said curtly she wasn't coming to the club that night. This hadn't happened before and I was nonplussed, stammering out an enquiry after her health.

'I'm quite alright, thank you. I just can't make it tonight,' she said, and put the phone down. Was she also sulking about what happened last Saturday? No, it was not her way, she enjoyed telling you outright what she thought. Could it be Marco's remark about my girlfriend?

I rang Marco, in the mood for going out now and unburdening myself. I had to face the fact that I wasn't an unqualified success when it came to women. Megan, Ewa, Vanessa - even Greta. Was I really the smug, controling, patronising, awkward guy they were collectively painting?

I got Marco's machine. I rang Ewa and got her machine. So I went out by myself and crawled a few neighbouring bars, talking to bartenders trying to restore some faith in my social capital. Woke up the next morning feeling as if I'd been hit by a bus, and lower than I'd been for several weeks.

After a couple of strong mugs of coffee which I'd learned to brew in the little metal percolator on the stove, I stumbled out to pick up some emails from a café down the street, to see if there were any comforting words from home. It was just a pile of the usual crap, most of which I deleted without opening. I was a bit of a demon deleter, sometimes at the expense of efficiency. I was just about to press the button on another sender I didn't recognise when something made my finger stop it mid air. I opened it. It said:

Dear Al,

You may be surprised to be receiving this from me after such a time, and you may not be pleased. I'd understand that, and couldn't blame you. But I hope we can at least talk to each other. I hope things are working out for you over there. Things haven't been going so well for me lately for one reason or another. I was wondering if you're thinking of coming home to Wales for Christmas? If so, would you consider going for a drink with me, for old time's sake if nothing else? If you don't want to, that's Ok too. I know I ignored you for a long time when you needed to talk to me.

Anyway, all the best.

Love, Megan.

Chapter Nine

Up to that point I hadn't given Christmas much thought. I had of course thought about Megan most waking days at some point, although by now I'd managed to abstract it somewhat, as something long ago and far away. I tried to avoid thinking of past events or future fantasies, so that it didn't hurt too much.

This email brought it all back with a blow so fierce I'm sure I must have swayed in my seat. I never had stopped feeling a twinge of excitement whenever she sent a text or called, or I heard her key in the front door. I cursed her for sending it, for setting back my recovery. In a strange way it sort of obliterated the last few months, or at least pushed them firmly in the shadow. It showed the power she had over me even now. I loved her still, in a way I didn't love Ewa. I admired Megan's self-assurance, her pluck, her chutzpah as Greta would probably have called it. Ewa, for all the carefree, fun-loving outside she liked to present to the world, had a certain sensitivity, even vulnerability about her that brought out my protective side, although I knew she would have found this deeply offensive. Now, with this one email from Megan, Ewa receded into the general blur of Manhattan, as hazy as a childhood memory. Almost before I got out of the chair I knew I would indeed be going back to Wales for Christmas, albeit with very little idea of what to expect.

I don't know how many times I must have read over the email, looking for clues or codes. It was certainly nothing like the bitch who said goodbye, so coolly, so cruelly, in that bar in the bay. It was more like the old Megan, or even like a new Megan; warmer, friendlier, more conciliatory than I can remember her even when we were first dating. Did it mean more than it said - or less?

As I walked back to the apartment, disorientated a little by the piercing winter morning sun which streamed down the street towards me, I ran through all the possibilities:

1) Megan meant what she wrote and simply wanted to meet again for old times' sake
2) She had an ulterior motive - money, something practical
3) She was lonely
4) She'd changed her mind (tried not to dwell on this one for too long for fear of endowing it with unrealistic hope, but it was as if I had to keep running my tongue over it like an aching tooth)
5) Something I hadn't thought of.

I came to the conclusion there was something I hadn't thought of. Could I think what I hadn't thought of?

My head was still swimming with all of this by the time I got back. I'd just flopped down in my old leather chair when the phone started ringing. It was Marco, insisting I joined him that evening for what he called his Speakeasy Tour. I was still in the throes of alcoholic remorse, the words Never Again swishing round my throbbing head. But this sounded too good to miss, would be a welcome distraction from all my woes, and allow me to postpone any reply to Megan's email until I'd talked it over with Marco.

The evening started off early, at six o'clock, with what Marco called a proper New York Bloody Mary, at a place he knew on Houston Street. It was an explosive mix replete with a celery stalk, Tabasco and a dollop of horseradish cream, served in a tall chunky tumbler. It wasn't so much a kick-start as a rocket-fuelled blast off.

We sat on high leather stools at the bar, Marco slouching over it with his usual slovenly elegance. I was just about to embark on the subject of Megan's email but before I knew it he whipped me out of the door, grabbed a cab and we were heading up to Union Square for the first real speakeasy, the Old Town Bar, which proclaimed itself as the oldest bar in town. It reeked of Old New York, all wooden booths, marble and glass. Marco ordered Michelobs and vodka shots, and we headed for one of the empty booths and sat down. He said the seats beneath us were in fact chests, which opened up for the storage of liquor bottles during prohibition. Of course I had to stand up and lift up the lid. Disappointingly, there were no old bottles of bootleg Bourbon underneath.

Here I did have the chance to lay out the whole situation. Marco listened patiently to the end - he could be a surprisingly good listener when he put his mind to it.

'Hmm,' he said finally, raising his eyebrows slightly. 'Come on, let's chew it over somewhere else'.

The next stop was Chumley's, one of the original speakeasies in New York, and had not Marco known it I doubt very much that I'd be able to find it, and don't think I'd be able to find it again. From the outside it looked like a villa in the Hispanic style with arches and tiles and no signs or lights to indicate anything out of the ordinary. The entrance was down a side alley which itself was difficult to find, then down a few steps like a cellar door. Inside it was so dark it took a couple of minutes for your eyes to adjust before you moved through the crowded tables to the dimly lit bar. More beer and vodka shots, and we found an empty table in the corner with a settle one side and a bench the other.

I was beginning to relax now, the world not looking so bad after al. Marco seemed reluctant to offer any opinion about my next steps with Megan, and I had to prise it out of him.

'Well, what do you think I should do about the email?' I asked with a tight-lipped grimace after a mouthful of neat vodka.

'You'll have to tell her you'll see her, of course.'

'Why 'Of course?"'

'It's what you've been waiting for.'

'No it isn't. It's what I've been dreading.'

I tried to convey how hard I'd worked to get to this stage where the mere thought of her did not bring on that old, searing pain, and that life was now just about bearable for the first time in months. He waved this aside.

'It's just what you told yourself to get through it. You weren't telling yourself the truth. You have to see her. You can't not. Then you'll know what the next step is.'

We ended the evening in the White Horse Tavern in Greenwich Village, where Dylan Thomas drank his legendary last, in the form of eighteen double whiskies. It made me think even more about going home for a Christmas in Wales. Marco clearly liked these old, atmospheric places. But by now it had all become somewhat hazy, I regret to have to report.

The next afternoon, a Sunday, I thought about Marco's words while carefully nursing a dreadful hangover. They were wise, I decided. I sat trying to compose a reply to Megan. It took several hours to achieve the effortlessly careless reply. I went through several drafts before I came up with this masterpiece.

Dear Megan,

I'm doing fine over here thanks. I'm sorry things haven't been so good for you. I probably will be in Cardiff over Christmas. Yes, let's meet up. Where would you suggest?

Al.

I'd just finished it when the phone rang. It was Mam with her regular Sunday call. She had a certain mournful voice she'd adopted for these brief transatlantic conversations as if I were in the trenches. But that day she sounded particularly low.

'It's your Dad,' she said. 'He's not well.'

'What is it?' I demanded.

'I don't want to discuss it over the phone. We can talk about it at Christmas.'

I pressed her but she refused to be drawn. I was angry that she left it hanging like that, letting my imagination do its worst. But I supposed that was Christmas decided.

No sooner had I put the phone down than it rang again. One of Ewa's favourites, *Double Indemnity*, was on TV that night. Why didn't I come over to watch it? We could order in some pizza. Great, I said, my heart not really in it. I could not now shake off this feeling that our relationship was proving more difficult than it should have been. We'd lost something of those early, easy-going days. It was as if we were circling warily around each other, unable to draw close.

When I got to her apartment I could see she'd made a bit of an effort. Smelly candles were flickering and a bottle of wine uncorked. A couple of menus were on the coffee table next to a huge bowl of popcorn. The movie was an excellent film noir. The illicit affair between a bored housewife and her husband's insurance agent ends with mutual destruction.

When it was over we talked about the relationship between Fred McMurray and Barbara Stanwyck. Could it have worked if they'd handled it differently, not resorted to murder? Ewa was curled up on the sofa, looking at me.

'And what about us? Where are we going?' she asked bluntly.

Well, at least it was out in the open. But I'm hopeless with this kind of Q&A, and it was even more difficult now that I had the meeting with Megan to come.

'I don't know,' I confessed, failing to grasp the nettle at the crucial moment. 'Isn't it too early to be asking these questions? We're just having a bit of fun, aren't we? Isn't that what we said we both wanted?'

'I'm not sure we are. There seems to be a distance lately. As soon as I think we're getting close you seem to move further back.'

That was exactly what I'd been thinking about her, but was it wise to say so?

'That's exactly what I've been thinking about you,' I said.

She abruptly changed the subject and asked, 'What are your plans for the Holidays?' as the Americans referred now to Christmas. A colleague at the faculty told me that a couple of years back they'd dumped the tradition of a Christmas party in favour of a Midwinter Solstice celebration, thinking it would be acceptable to all creeds. But they got a complaint from a fully paid up Pagan saying they were dissing her festival. So this year they were throwing in the towel and had gone for a Miami Beach Party with deck chairs, palm trees and cocktails with parasols.

'I'm going back to Wales.'

'I thought we could do something together. Go up to Vermont and do a bit of skiing. What about New Year's?'

'Well, it's a long journey back to my neck of the woods, so I'll probably spend the two weeks' vacation there,' I said, feeling a bit of a heel but thinking of that date with Megan…..

Ewa got up and looked out of the window in silence for a moment or two. When she'd regained her composure she turned back into the room and walked towards me, sitting down close to me on the sofa.

'If I seem a little distant at times, it's because I've been hurt in the past. My independence is hard won and I'm not about to give it up now.'

'That's exactly what I've been trying to do, not threaten your independence'.

'But you *are* threatening me. You want everything on your terms. There's your inviolable Tuesday and Friday nights. Nothing can interfere with that. I seem to take second place.'

'Can you tell me how you've been hurt?'

'Oh no, Al, I don't want to rake it back all over again. I've put my trust in men in the past and they've betrayed me. Let's leave it at that.'

So she *was* jealous of the Bridge Club. I suggested maybe we were dancing around each other too much, forgetting how much fun we used to have when things were less complicated.

'And I'm not getting any younger,' she said almost wistfully, which was very unlike her. She wasn't even thirty. 'I can't help feeling that time is running out, that I can take fewer risks. I don't want to feel this way, but I do.'

Was she thinking about having babies? About *us* having babies? But now she'd got this off her chest it did seem to clear the air somewhat, and we both remembered some of the good times. It was as if we weren't quite sure what we had, even less sure of what we would have, but we didn't want to let it go.

We snuggled up and had some more wine. She stayed that night and we made love, very good love. In the morning we were almost *in* love. We made bacon and eggs and were appreciative of each other, attentive. Yet in the back of my mind was that email I'd sent to Megan.

Megan and I exchanged a couple of emails in the week, trying to pin down where we'd meet, both of us instinctively wanting to avoid all the old familiar places that held too many awkward memories. She struggled to find a new one - Cardiff is a fairly small place after all. I suggested a restaurant but she ruled this out. I suspected she thought this would pin us down too much, commit us to sitting down and facing each other in a formal setting, and she was probably right. She didn't want to drive out of town, probably because she figured both of us would need a couple of drinks, and taxis would involve more waiting and rigmarole. Clearly any of our friends' or relations' places were out of the question. In the end she proposed a new bar in Canton, a part of town we didn't know so well and which was apparently picking itself up and dusting itself off from its reputation as Boozers and Junkies Central.

December 29th, eight o'clock, she said. I could tell something must be quite wrong for her to tear herself away from her beloved circle of friends and round of festive parties. In the middle of the week, as if to rub in all my confusion, Ewa rang me at work, something she hardly ever did, and suggested lunch in the cafeteria. My heart did quicken at this, and when I saw her sitting over by the window it leapt. Ewa was relaxed, seemed to want to make a fresh start. She'd rang on impulse. The fact that we were meeting in a faculty dining hall gave it an illicit, exciting edge, and we couldn't help smiling at the half-whispered, intimate moments like young lovers. It felt as if some kind of corner had been turned.

By Friday I'd almost forgotten about Greta and Bridge. I'd gone back to my apartment after classes and was napping in my favourite - well, in fact only - armchair, the cracked leather one found in the street a couple of blocks away. Suddenly it dawned on me what day of the week it was and I leapt out of it to call Greta, but the phone started ringing before I reached it.

'Just checking you're not going to let me down tonight,' she said, as if there'd been no cooling off between us. It was only in her eagerness to play that she showed the slightest hint of vulnerability, of neediness, But even now that 'let me down' could turn it into an accusation. She must have called from the New Cavendish. She always got there early and it was nearly seven o'clock - I had only half an hour or so to get up there. I dashed out, just grabbing my coat from the hooks by the door and ran out into the street, loudly hailing a cab that had just passed.

Even so it would be touch and go whether I made it in time. Greta would have found another partner if I didn't, possibly never to play with me again. My heart was in my mouth all the way uptown, and I couldn't help leaning forward in my seat so that a couple of times when the driver braked at lights my nose bumped the plastic divider between front and back. I kept telling myself it was ridiculous to be behaving as if it were a matter of life and death

For once the traffic and the lights were in my favour and the cab screeched to a halt outside the club at twenty five past. I ran to the elevator and just about caught my breath on the way up. Greta was sitting there opposite an empty chair, drumming her fingers on the green baize.

'Well, well,' she said, turning her head slowly towards me in that spooky way of hers, 'look who's turned up.'

But she was smiling her stiff smile. She was the girlish, excited Greta, and I knew instantly she was up to something. The play began straightaway - our opponents were already in place - so I would have to wait to find out what.

We did well in the first few rounds, effortlessly finding a few 3NT contracts which was Greta's favourite and had become mine. Over the last few months Greta had taught me well, if a little impatiently at times, and now we had a good understanding. I was making fewer and fewer mistakes, and at least now often knew when I had made one. Other, better players were more ambitious and had an array of conventions at their command all with those exotic names - Sputnik, Lundy, Roman Key Card Blackwood. But these would not come into play all that often and so they sometimes went wrong, disastrously so. Greta and I were steadier players, held our course and stuck to what we knew. As Greta said, nothing fancy.

As East and West got up from the table towards the end of the session, Greta bestowed me with a gracious look.

'There's a tournament here tomorrow,' she announced, 'and I think you're ready for it.'

I was flattered, but had a vague arrangement to see Ewa. I tried to wriggle out of it by protesting that I was not up to it, would be too nervous, which was also true. In a tournament you're playing against people from other clubs and some of the best players in New York would turn out. But Greta was having none of it. It was a Royal Command.

'Nonsense.' It was one of her favourite words which she pronounced as two separate ones: none sense. 'I'm the best judge of whether you're up to it or not. It starts at twelve. There'll be good food here. You'll enjoy it.'

When I opened the blinds the next morning there was quite a thick covering of snow on the various roofs, decks and yards I could see through my window. I went out into the hall and looked into the street. The snow was also thick where the gritters had not been able to reach. I called Greta hoping that the weather would put her off, but I should have known better.

'I'll take a cab', she said. She usually drove her huge grey Lincoln across the park in a stately, not to say snail-paced manner as if she'd strayed from a funeral procession, which wouldn't have been surprising as she could barely see over the dashboard.

'How long do you think it'll go on for?'

'We'll be through by about seven. Make sure you leave in plenty of time,' and I was dismissed with a hang-up click.

I called Ewa. I thought we were probably meant to be doing something that afternoon, but suggested we had dinner later on. Ewa readily and happily agreed to this, thank God, as if she'd had the same thought. But it didn't stop me from feeling, I don't know - underhand.

When I got there Greta was already in her usual seat, in her element, which in her case was not always a good thing. She clearly felt in control, and was even more dictatorial than usual, ordering me to go up and get a plateful of food form the buffet before the line grew too long, and to bring one back for her to precise specifications. I'd never known Greta to be a big eater and indeed she didn't ask for much for herself, but it was as if she was greedy on my behalf, egging me on to stack my plate.

The food was certainly plentiful: bagel sandwiches towering with countless layers, platters of cold meats and pickles, bowls of salads, boards of cheese and crackers, dishes of fruit and trays of fancy cakes and cookies.

My old nerves came back with a vengeance, to the extent that my hands were shaking as I sorted out my cards into suits for the first hand. I suppose it was a sign of how relaxed I'd become playing with Greta on Friday nights. The place was packed, every table occupied, and the atmosphere was far more tense than in a normal game. The excited hum turned to a hush as people finished eating and took their places. Then I discovered the reason, I thought, for Greta's mischievous glee.

'There's a world champion here,' Greta announced in a would-be nonchalant way.

'Who?'

'Sophie Weber.'

'Where,' I asked, startled, looking around.

'I can't see her,' said Greta. 'She must be in the other room.'

'Is she playing East or West?' was my next question. If she was, that would mean we'd probably play against her.

'I don't know,' said Greta, feigning disinterest.

I managed to calm down slightly as play proceeded, but if I thought I'd made a lot of progress in recent weeks I was in for an unpleasant surprise. We didn't make any catastrophic mistakes, but we, or I should say I, seemed unequal to many of the players. We just couldn't do anything against them. I'd grown quite confident in my game, and now it was if I knew nothing at all, indeed had gone backwards.

At one point I must have hesitated for too long over a particularly difficult bid. This apparently could inform my partner that I was at least strong enough to consider bidding further, and East called the Director on me, as was their right. The Director, a thin, stern guy with a bow tie, came over and listened to East's complaint. In the end he did not give me any penalties (he could have taken a trick off us, or even awarded the game to the opponents) but told me to speed up my bidding. My hands started shaking again.

Oddly enough, Greta kept her composure throughout the afternoon and even seemed to be enjoying the proceedings. The thought briefly crossed my mind that she had foreseen the whole thing, knew that I was not really up to this and thought she'd bring me down a peg or two. But no, not even Greta could be that calculating, could she? And surely she wouldn't endure this humiliation just to get one over on me?

'Here she comes,' said Greta, towards the end of the afternoon. I looked up and saw two well-groomed, elegant women in their forties approach our table. Greta nodded towards the taller of the two, who I figured must be the World Champion. She wore glasses and had short blond hair. She looked pleasant and not as aloof as many of the other players.

They sat down and smiled at us. It was Greta's opening bid. She bid one spade. The Champ on my right passed. I looked at my hand. I had twelve points, and five spades. This was at the top end of what's known as a limit raise, where you raise your partner's bid to three of her suit. It means you have ten to twelve points and support for your partner's suit. But given that I had five in her suit, should I go straight to game and say four spades? I reasoned that raising her to four was a weaker bid, just promising spades and not a lot of points. It was something of a shut-out bid, denying her the chance to go further and look for a slam. And all my points were in aces in the other suits - aces and spaces - which can somewhat devalue your hand.

'Three spades,' I said firmly. There were three passes, so the World

Champ led a card, and I laid my hand down.

The Champ raised her eyebrows.

'That wasn't very brave of you,' she said with a smile.

Greta glared. 'You should have gone four spades,' she said, her mouth curling up in scorn. 'Well, he is within the limit of the limit raise,' said East in my defence.

In the end, it only made three spades, through no fault of Greta's. Four spades just wasn't there. It's like that sometimes. Even if a game should be makable in theory, it doesn't necessarily work out in practice. A bit like Megan and me, I couldn't help thinking.

Greta took the little score sheet from its slot on the bottom of the card tray and opened it. We all craned to see the other scores. All the other tables had ended up in four spades, and had all gone one trick down, so Greta and I had a top score against the World Champion.

'Well done,' said Sophie Weber with another of her charming smiles. 'You were right after all.'

Greta continued to glare. I was right and she was wrong, which was obviously not a satisfactory state of affairs. But we both knew it was a hollow victory, a fluke. It was the bright spot in a gloomy game. I don't think we came bottom, but we weren't far off.

'Well, did you enjoy that?' she asked, with something that was not quite a smile as we got up to go. I could tell she was disappointed - with me, with the whole afternoon.

'Uh, sort of. It was a bit nerve-wracking. I'm sorry If I didn't come up to scratch.'

'Well, this *is* a tournament you know.' As if I'd forgotten. As if I only had myself to blame. 'It's a different standard of play here. Some of the top players are out. And you've got to start some time.'

As we were going out, I saw Sandra, and noticed that Greta cold-shouldered her. I hung back a little and asked her, 'Isn't Greta speaking to you?'

'No, I don't think so,' and it was the first time I'd seen this friendly, fluffy old woman looking grim-faced and downcast.

'Why not?'

'Because she's a Sonofabitch. Pardon my French'.

'Well, it's her loss,' I said.

She gave me a sad little smile.

How cruel the woman was. Finding her One Good Thing seemed to be an increasingly remote prospect.

Chapter Ten

The first thing to strike me when I got back to Wales on Christmas Eve was how small, neat and clean everything looked. I'd noticed this even from the runway at Heathrow when the overnight from JFK touched down, but it was even more pronounced in Wales. I was surprised because I'd never thought of Britain as a particularly clean country. And I enjoyed the train journey down to Cardiff, viewing the countryside and towns through new eyes.

It relaxed me a little, for I was a jumble of emotions. I'd managed to sleep a little on the flight, after a few beers and a sleeping pill, so I was woozy. But also excited and nervous about seeing friends and family again, not to mention anxious about meeting Megan after all this time, not knowing what to expect.

And then it came to me in a flash and I think I must have sat up bolt upright in my seat. Divorce. Of course. She wanted a divorce. That was the one thing I couldn't think of when I ran through the options of what she wanted, probably because I didn't want to think about it. Strangely enough the word had never cropped up. When she dumped me so unceremoniously on that grim night in the Bay, we didn't even get to it. As far as I could recall, the nearest we came to it was talking about a trial separation, but as we both surely knew the only part of separation that was a trial was the ordeal itself. We'd had enough friends go through one to know that it was little more than sugar on the pill of termination. If it was a trial, the verdict was more or less a foregone conclusion: there would be no going back.

Why hadn't I seen this before? She simply wanted to sit down and discuss the terms of a divorce. She'd kept on our house, but we'd made no provision for a permanent ending.

But was that the way it was done? Wouldn't I have just received a snippy letter from a fortune-grabbing lawyer? Maybe that wasn't Megan's way. How could I tell? By the time the train reached the Severn Tunnel, I was certain that this was what I was going back to. Maybe somewhere in the back of my mind, without being aware of it even, I'd begun to think I could just go back to where we left off. My heart was now beating at the thought of such finality. Yet finality was what I'd been telling myself I needed, an end to this hellish limbo that had all but cracked me up in the first place. After that night in the Bay, I now realised, I'd somehow got to thinking that if I couldn't go on living with her, having her in my life, then at least the second best thing was eventually to have some kind of friendly relationship. But after what I'd been through I could see that second best wasn't settling for a greatly diluted form of the best thing. Second best was finality, an end to turmoil, so I could, in common parlance - very common in America - have closure. Now I was confronted with the prospect I felt scared all over again.

I thought back to my life in New York, which was rapidly taking on the quality of a dream. Could I go back to that? Could I make it my new life? I was enjoying the lecturing, and secretly knew I was popular. Even though at first I missed the edgier, cheekier students in Cardiff, I'd begun to get used to those in New York. And I thought they'd begun to get used to me and my strange sense of humour. And there were some who kept me on my toes. One called Mikel who came from Harlem was vociferously proud of his roots and saw mainstream journalism as a subliminal conspiracy to keep power in the hands of the powerful. I agreed with many of his views.

He would saunter in to class about half an hour late. Eventually I'd had enough and pulled him aside.

'I've been to my grandmother's funeral,' he said.

'How many grandmothers do you have, Mikel? You've buried at least two so far this year to my knowledge.'

He gave a sly smile as if to say he was up for this game.

'Well, she was my great aunt really but we called her grandma. You know how it is.' He knew full well that I didn't know how it was with his family. 'And look, I'm all in black.'

'You're always all in black,' I said. 'Go and sit down. And Mikel....'

'Yes?'

'Do try to look after your remaining grandmothers better. And come to class on time.'

He grinned broadly at this, so I could tell the grandmother story was a shtick and one he usually got away with. His time-keeping did improve after that.

Vanessa and I were working well together, despite her occasional flare-ups, as I thought of them. Something told me that, despite her outward pride in her Welsh ancestry, she resented the Brits and the fact that I was teaching her subject to Americans. I'd tried to figure out why this should be. Maybe some grievance about our colonial past, or the arrogance she perceived in the Brits, or our prior claim on the language. Again, I could sympathise to a certain extent.

The Bridge had continued, with Greta blowing hot and cold, unfathomable, infuriating. When I told her I was coming back to Wales for Christmas, she did deign to say she'd miss me, and asked me if I could bring her back some perfume, a particular kind by Oscar de la Renta.

Ewa and I had been getting on well since that heart to heart. She seemed to have decided to trust me, to let me penetrate that defensive shield of hers. We started enjoying our times together again, and I tried not to appear too pre-occupied, as at times no doubt I was after the emails with Megan began. I'd tried to tell myself the exchanges changed nothing, but it didn't work. Megan had come to dominate my thoughts again, damn her, just when I thought I was beginning to break free. It was like going back to smoking after quitting.

Marco was a good buddy but his own man, often out of town on assignments, so there were limits to our friendship. Did all this add up to reasons for prolonging my stay, which would probably be easy enough? On paper, definitely not.

By the time I reached journey's end I was exhausted with these conundrums. As I stepped down from the train I had to draw a deep breath to prepare myself for the evening ahead. Dad was at Cardiff Central to meet me, standing by the car in the little parking bay in front. We shook hands awkwardly, not quite knowing whether to hug. We ended up doing a handshake and half hug at the same time, chins resting briefly on shoulders.

We were both fairly quiet as we drove through town. I was preoccupied with his health problems that Mam had hinted at. I wished he'd ask me lots of questions about New York, and didn't want to volunteer too much information. St Mary's Street looked festive, packed with bustling, merry shoppers. It was hardly the Rockefeller Center, but all the better for it. There was some sleet in the wind and the hilltops beyond the city had a sprinkling of white. I enjoyed the drive up to Taff's Well, just north of the city, where Mam and Dad had their semi. There was a scattering of snow on the hills. Everything looked familiar, but at the same time different.

Mam was in the kitchen when we arrived, poring over lists of things she had to do, and gave me a half hug with floury hands waving in the air. She looked older, ill somehow, her hair greyer and her face almost as white as her hands behind a mask of festivity. They'd got the house done up for my sister's two kids – they were all staying too so it would be a bit of a squeeze. I recognised some of the old decorations we'd had as kids, and some new ones. Memories of childhood Christmases infused the whole atmosphere, like an long-forgotten song or the smell of French cigarettes.

It would be a lot of work for Mam but she insisted she'd enjoy it if we all mucked in. We all sat down to sausage and mash and onion gravy and a bottle of wine, which had only recently become standard in the house when they had company. It was Kath and her husband Mike who asked most of the questions about my life in New York while Mam and Dad listened on. I felt unsettled, antsy as the Americans would say, something apart from the Megan thing. Coming back here was good in a way, but at the back of my mind were dark thoughts about how dowdy it all was, how bourgeois and ordinary after my escapades in New York.

I tried to put these thoughts to the back of my mind and appreciate instead the warmth surrounding me, but they'd creep back when I wasn't looking. It wasn't so much that I was rejecting this life, but I couldn't wholly accept it either. The last thing I wanted was for them to realise this. Naturally they would be protective of their own lives, defensive even. I had to concede to myself though something I'd never conceded before – that maybe I'd always found their life drab. In half-remembered childhood trips to see my grandparents in Mid-Wales or the Rhondda, I'd always found their lives more exciting, romantic than my own upbringing, although even at that young age something told me this must be far from the truth. My thoughts flew back to Ewa, and her own restless pursuit of ancestral anecdotes.

Dad made a great show of jumping up as soon as we'd finished eating and roping me in to do the washing up with him. It all felt a little strange. As soon as that was over, he insisted we went down to the local, but I can't say I offered much resistance. It was quite strained for us all being cooped up in the house. He must have hoped we'd all feel a little more at home in the pub. He would, anyway. Kath said the men could go, she didn't mind, but Mam wanted us all out of the house so she could 'get on'. She'd look after the kids.

While Dad was upstairs getting changed, Mam beckoned Kath and me into the kitchen.

'I've already told Kath,' she begun. 'The doctor's told me Dad's got an aneurysm in his aorta - that's a little bulge in the main vein from his heart. There are no real symptoms and nothing to be done about it. He could go on for years as he is but……he could go at any minute. The question is, do we tell him or not? The doctor said it was up to us.'

She made her little speech in a matter-of-fact tone, without a single stumble. I took a deep breath and looked at Kath who was looking at me expectantly.

'What do you think?' I asked.

'You first. I've told Mam what I think. I want you to give your own opinion.'

I knew immediately what I would say.

'I don't think there's any point in telling him if there's nothing to be done. He's enjoying life - why cloud it? I'm sure if it was me I wouldn't want to know.'

'That's what I said,' said Kath with relief.

'Right. We're all agreed then,' said Mam. 'Let's hear no more about it. Now off you all go down the pub. I've got my jobs to do. Go on. Shoo! Shoo!' She waved her tea cloth at us as if we were chickens.

The pub was packed and it was clear that many people had made an afternoon of it. It was odd stepping back into such a culture of drinking. Marco aside, it wasn't the same in New York. But we all soon got into the spirit of things. There was quite a bit of ribbing about my fancy New York ways. When I went to the bar with Dad to get the first round, he pulled me up for saying 'Can I get a....' instead of 'Could I have a.....' I'd thought I'd been prepared for this and had told myself not to do or say anything that could be construed as getting above myself - a cardinal sin in Wales. If I did, I knew I'd be brought back down to earth with a bump. My Gran used to tell us of the woman who lived at the end of their terrace in the Rhondda. She considered herself a cut above because of this - they had a stairs window in the end wall and steps leading up to the front door as the street sloped down the valley. She was always out washing them, as women did in those days, and was known as Mrs Two Steps, for that's all there were. I believed I'd been assiduous in avoiding Americanisms, but some were unavoidable. If you said to-mah-toe, for example, you could have a hard time being understood. I'd slipped quite easily into tuh-meh-toe. Gas was another one, for petrol. And wind for that matter.

I think Dad was proud of me in a way, venturing so far afield, as long as I didn't forget my roots. The Valleys people prided themselves on being matter-of-fact, down to earth, I reflected, especially in unusual situations. I thought of that old joke. The valley was flooded, and the Jones family were sitting patiently on the roof of their house, water lapping round their feet. A rowboat approached and someone shouted out through a megaphone, 'We're the Red Cross.' Mrs Jones cupped her hands round her mouth and shouted back, 'We already gave.'

We managed to be jolly but now and again I caught myself looking at Dad with affection, and once I'm sure he caught me doing it. I wondered if he knew more than he was letting on.

'So what've you been doing for fun in the Big Apple?' he asked, bringing me out of myself.

'As a matter of fact, I've been playing quite a lot of Bridge'.

'Bridge? That's a good one.'

'No, seriously, I have. I'm almost a Club Master now'.

It was true. Greta and I had been racking up the points and I'd already reached Junior Master level. We only needed two or three more placings for me to become Club Master.

'Good for you', said Kath, clinking her glass on mine. I suddenly remembered that it was her suggestion in the first place.

'And I have you to thank for it,' I said, clinking mine back. Dad and Mike started to shuffle their way to the bar to get another round in. 'It was a bit of a lifesaver,' I said to Kath in a lower voice. 'Took me out of myself'.

'I'm glad. Something had to. Any word from....Uh...?' Funny how people think they're being more sensitive if they don't mention people's names.

'Well, Uh and I have exchanged a couple of emails. That's about it'. I couldn't bring myself to tell her an outright lie, but wanted to leave it at that for the time being, and I knew she'd understand. The whole family were still a little in denial about our break-up, but were discreet and supportive enough not to ask too many questions or interfere too much. But I also knew there was a lot they wanted to know, that perhaps I should tell them. I was worried that I was creating a kind of tension that might spoil their Christmas.

'Have any of you heard anything from her?' I asked.

'Not a word', said Kath, a little regretfully I thought.

Christmas, I have to say, was wonderful. Like most lucky children brought up in fairly bountiful homes, I'd loved Christmas when I was a kid, but in recent years it had just become an endless round of parties. It made it special again having the kids around. We'd all piled presents under the tree as we did when we were kids, to be opened after Christmas dinner.

Mam had got up at the crack of dawn to put the monstrous turkey in the oven and Aled and Anwen squealed the rest of us awake soon after. They had football socks tied to their bunk beds which they were allowed to open when they woke up,

Under Mam's supervision we peeled spuds, scraped carrots, scored sprouts, pricked sausages. Even Dad hung around the kitchen, getting in everyone's way, offering his services as limited as they were. He was given simple tasks like washing up as we went along and dishing out sauces into designated dishes. By about 11.30 everything was under control and the whisky and sherry bottles were brought out as we congratulated each other on jobs well done and drank to the season.

Mike offered to keep things bubbling along while Mam, Dad, Kath and I strolled down the hill to the pub again for the ritual couple of Christmas lunchtime drinks. It was bitterly cold now, and the hills were whiter than yesterday.

Now that the back of the work was broken, Mam relaxed and ordered large G&Ts to keep up with us, and the four of us slipped into a chatty, jokey hour or so which I think did us all good. I relaxed too, forgetting about my own troubles and what was ahead of me. There was a guy there with a guitar - just a local who brought it along. He was good and soon got the entire pub singing favourite carols. Then he played an action song called something like The Music Master: *I am the music master, and I can play my pia- pia- piano, piano, piano.....* The next verse added *picco- picco- piccolo, piccolo, piccolo.* Soon we were adding the Archer's theme tune, the Dambusters' music and so on. Vanessa would have approved. You couldn't have ordered a better Christmas drink.

We staggered up the hill, me clutching Mam and Kath clutching Dad., light snow now flurrying down. Mike had everything under control back at the house, even the excited kids, more or less. Christmas dinner was jovial and carefree, wine and talk flowed, everyone sang Mam's praises and she glowed but made light of it. The presents were ripped open frenetically by the kids and more languidly by the rest of us. I got a smart Bridge set from Kath and a suit carrier from Mam and Dad – Mam still fondly believed I wore suits to work. The presents I'd bought from Bloomingdales went over well, without undue comment about my swankiness. We sat down to doze through the Queen's speech while the kids played with their toys. I marvelled at the normalcy of it all.

Boxing Day was spent traditionally with cold meats and cider, even for the kids, despite their father's protests. Dad clung to his lifelong belief that cider was not really alcoholic. Then a green baize cloth was found in a drawer of the dresser and the four of us played whist. Mam told us about the time her mother won an entire Christmas dinner – turkey, veg, cake and pudding – at various whist drives. As we were playing, I asked Mam to tell us more about life on the farm.

'What do you want to know?'

'Well, what were Christmases like?'

'Not nearly as commercial as now, for one thing. You used what you had. You didn't buy much in. My mother would sell ducks for her Christmas purse, as she put it. Why are you asking now, anyway? I brought you up on stories of the farm. You were never that interested.'

'I'm interested now.'

'Well, it's difficult just to come out with them to order. My mother had loads of old sayings, particularly about predicting the weather. One of them was "Frost in November to hold a duck, nothing after but slush and muck." I was never all that interested in them when I was young either, and anyway your Gran didn't want me to pay much heed to the old ways. She wanted me to look forward, move on, make the most of the chances she never had.

'Well, just before she died, I thought I'd get her to write all these sayings down. I thought I could use them in school. Oral history was becoming all the rage then. They'd never much bothered with the lives of ordinary people before. So she did. But when she handed me two or three pages of notepaper I saw the first one was "a stitch in time saves nine." And so it went on. They were all everyday proverbs that we all know. None of the old country ones. I didn't have the heart to tell her they weren't what I wanted. I suppose I should have listened to them when I had the chance. But the point is, it's hard for people to come up with old memories when you put them on the spot. Something has to trigger it off.'

'Duw, I remember the Christmases in the Rhondda in the thirties,' said Dad, as if to prove the point. 'Times were hard.'

We'd all heard this many times before, but listened politely.

'We were lucky if we got an apple and an orange and one little toy in our stockings. We'd go up the mountain on Christmas Eve to get a little pine, and decorate it with chains we made from coloured paper.'

'What's sparked off this sudden curiosity about the past?' asked Mam.

I told them about Ellis Island, without mentioning Ewa, and about Greta – how I wondered what had happened in her past to make her so nasty.

'Well, it's going to be no easy task to get to the bottom of that,' said Mam.

Kath and family left the next morning, and I suggested we go for a drive up to the Rhondda. Mam said she was too busy and would be glad of a bit of time to herself, so told us to go. I asked Dad if we could drive up to Hirwaun and go over the top to the valley. The drive had special memories for me. It was the way Dad used to take us as kids to see our grandparents. The tops of the slag heaps always seemed to be cloaked in swirling mist, and as you wound down to the valley floor the mist gave way to smoking chimneys, which invested it all with a majestic, almost biblical aura.

The snow had almost cleared but the small open road over the mountains was still a little treacherous, adding that little thrill of peril that I used to dread and love. The mines had now all gone, of course, and the valley had undergone a remarkable transformation, like Llewellyn's sequel *Green, Green My Valley Now.* Pity it came at such a price.

The terraces still snaked around the curves of the mountains, but as we headed down to Gelli Road, the loss of industry was obvious and the streets had a neglected, down-at-heel air. I looked at Dad and saw him looking around forlornly.

'Duw, it's changed, mun,' he said, slipping automatically back into the vernacular.

'How was it when you were kids?'

'Dunno. Basic but thriving, if you get me. There was work in the pits. We were close-knit. We made do. We used to get cardboard boxes from the shoe shop, and go up the mountain and slide down the slag heaps. We didn't know any better. To us it was as good as winter sports. Then we'd damn the Waun to make a paddling pool. You could always find something to do.'

I waited for more.

'And then we'd play cricket or have races in the gwlis.'

'Goolies?'

'Gwlis, mun. The back lanes behind the houses. Comes from gullies, I suppose. There were always sheep everywhere. We used to get them to play silly mid-off.' He winked. 'They used to say the sheep had learnt to roll over the cattle grids to come down off the mountain and raid our bins.'

'I remember Gran's famous Sunday roasts,' I said. 'We'd all be cramped in the back kitchen. She'd ask if you wanted more at the same time putting huge dollops of mashed potato on your plate whether you said yes or not.'

'Aye. Middle room for best, front room for funerals. They used to know her round here as Maisie Chops, you know.'

'Why?'

'Well because she was always chopsing. Never stopped talking.'

'Did she know?'

'Oh, probably. But she never let on.'

We parked the car in a little car park and walked to the house. It was still there, looking much smaller of course, but it was comforting to see. We walked round the gwli and on the corner was the Working Men's Club where my grandfather must have drank. It had seen better days. The memories were so real, like a drowned village re-emerging from a drought-stricken reservoir.

The streets stretched endlessly down the valley. But to the people who lived there each village was distinct. I recalled my cousins talking about going to see Semprini (sounded wonderful in their melodic Rhondda accents) in a concert.

'Is that near here?' I'd asked.

'Nooo,' said Meryl incredulously. 'Tonypandy.' It was about three streets away.

'Do you regret leaving here?' I asked Dad as we got back in the car.

'Good God, no. It was a tough life, and people were pleased for you to go. It's got a pull though - the people are so distinctive with their way of talking and their own brand of humour. But I have little time for regret, and you can't go back.'

His words struck an ominous chord. I was due to meet Megan the next night. I told my parents I was going to meet some friends. I had to use the plural otherwise Mam would ask who it was. It had been a great Christmas, but now it was time to face reality, the past, the future....

I got to the bar in plenty of time, so she wouldn't have to wait there alone, which wouldn't go down very well. I got a beer, just stopping myself in time from tipping the barman, and sat in a booth near the window so I could see her as soon as she walked in. The place was done up in the latest style: dark purple walls, black and white photos of old Cardiff in large black wooden frames lit by overhanging brass lamps, dark brown leather chairs and wooden benches.

She was pretty punctual too. As she walked in she looked less sure of herself than she used to, and a little haggard, as if she had a cold or hadn't slept. She was in her familiar black, her hair cropped short. She had a lit cigarette in her hand. I stood up and she spotted me.

'Hello Al.'

'Hello Megan.'

We didn't kiss. I went over to the bar to get her vodka and tonic. As I was waiting I sneaked a couple of looks at her. She didn't look happy. When I rejoined her we were silent for a few moments. It was so difficult to know where to begin.

'So how've you been?' she asked eventually. 'You're looking well.'

'Oh, not too bad. Good to get away to New York. New start and all that. You?'

'Oh, OK.'

We sipped our drinks, staring ahead of us.

'Well, actually, not so OK.'

'Oh?'

'Haven't been getting along as well as I thought I would.'

'I'm sorry to hear that,' I said, managing to keep a tinge of irony out of my voice.

'Al, I may as well come straight to the point. I think I made a mistake. I don't know what came over me. Going through some kind of crisis, I suppose. I miss you, Al.'

I almost spat out my beer. The first thing I felt was anger.

'I don't know what to say,' I said. 'I've struggled so hard to put it all behind me. How can you play with me like this? I've had to turn my life round completely. Are you sure you're not making a mistake now?'

'You're going to have to trust me, Al. I'm just being honest.'

'I'm not sure I can ever really trust you again.' It was a cheap shot. Cruel. But I wanted to be cruel, give her a taste of her own medicine. I wasn't big enough to pass up the opportunity. And I was disappointed in myself. She lit up another of her long brown cigarettes.

'I understand that. But I mean what I say. Do you think we could give it another go?' she asked in a small voice.

'Just like that?'

'Like what, then?'

'You're going to have to give me some time to think things over.'

'Oh yes, I knew that.'

'But what were you feeling when you dumped me?'

'I suppose I was feeling trapped, as if life was passing me by.'

'What made you change your mind?' I asked severely.

'Oh, I don't know.' She looked away to brush a tear.

'Actually, I do in a way.' She took a sip for courage. 'I'm ill, Al.'

'Ill? What is it?'

'Breast cancer.'

The anger vanished.

'Are you going to be alright?'

'Oh, yes, I think so. I'll have to have an op in a month. I wasn't going to tell you. Didn't want you to feel sorry for me, or think I was playing the Camille card to get you back, after all I put you through. But I see now that I couldn't keep it from you. It would be wrong.'

I reached out and took her hand.

'Believe me, I *am* sorry for what I did. I didn't even know what I wanted. But this wretched thing has made me see things more clearly. I think I know what I want now Al. It's you. It's you in my life. You *and* my life.'

I moved over to her side of the booth. We hugged and held hands.

'Are you thinking of coming back to Cardiff?'

'Don't know yet. As I say, I went to make a new life for myself. You can't do that overnight. I still think I should give it a chance.'

'If you did come back,' she said slowly, 'do you think we could have another go at it? Have a sort of trial?'

I gave what I thought would be a noncommittal yet comforting answer. We stayed until closing time, catching up on old friends, telling each other about our separate lives. We arranged to see each other again in a few days, before I went back to New York. She didn't press me for an answer by then, but I knew it was only fair to give her some indication. I put her in a taxi. She was weeping a little again.

'You going to be alright?'

'Yes, I'm going to be alright,' she said, smiling through her tears. 'I'm so sorry, Al.'

The next few days I was, to say the least, a little distracted. I think Mam noticed but didn't ask any awkward questions. I saw a couple of old friends, but didn't want to talk this over with them, not even with Nick. In fact I thought of Marco. What would he say? I knew what he'd say. Could I find it in myself to trust Megan again, to put the past behind me? Part of me had cast her in a new light, giving her a harder, selfish, uncaring edge which I didn't like. But people do have bad times, mad moments, don't they? Maybe it was part of her illness, even. She'd apologised, admitted her mistake. Was there indeed anything to think over?

We were to meet in the same bar three days later. Again I was in plenty of time, but this time Megan was already there, sitting in the same booth, playing with a drink. She looked different, kind of more hopeful, I guess, especially as she looked up to greet me.

I still hadn't worked out in my mind exactly what I was going to say, but I knew I'd have to say it soon.

'I've been thinking about what you said,' I began. 'I must say it came as a bit of a shock.'

She sat there patiently.

'I'm going back to New York and see the year out. I've begun to quite enjoy the teaching now. I hadn't really thought beyond that. I suppose I could get the year extended if I wanted to. But if I do come back, I would like to give it another go, Megan. I don't think I could ever love anyone as much as I love you.'

She gave a tiny sob, and I struggled not to.

'Thank you, Al. Thank you. You can't know how much it means to me that you've forgiven me. God knows I don't deserve it. It's almost enough.'

'Let's keep in touch and that'll give us time to get used to the idea again.'

'I do understand that you'll need time. But just so you know, I don't. I've had my moment of madness. It's over.'

I still couldn't be sure of that. I remembered her saying it was over once before. My fear was that she'd change her mind again, especially if the operation went well. Maybe that was a mean thing to think, but I couldn't help it. I didn't say it though. I think Megan had got the message. My next dilemma was what to say to Ewa when I got back to New York.

Chapter Eleven

When I walked back into the New Cavendish, the place looked different somehow, more cheerful. But it must have been I who was more cheerful, and the room was now simply free of my misery. The hurt of rejection was still there, but it felt like it was healing after Megan admitting it was all a mistake.

I found Greta on her throne, beaming serenely.

'I've missed you,' she said, and clasped her hand on mine as she sat down. I was glad I remembered her perfume, and handed it over.

'Oh, thank you so much. What do I owe you?'

'Please, it's a gift.' I was in a good mood too.

Greta seemed genuinely delighted, the first time I'd seen her like this.

'It's a gift,' I heard in a whispered exclamation just behind me. I turned round and saw Lily on the next table, in the black sweater covered with coloured sequins. Sandra was sitting opposite her, and they were both looking our way. So the question of whether the perfume was a gift had become something of a news item. No doubt Greta had been blabbing that I was bringing her back some expensive perfume. I wondered they couldn't find anything more interesting to talk about, and had not realised such an interest was taken in our affairs, beyond the widespread surprise that I had stayed Greta's partner for so long. I saw now that we must have struck people as quite an odd pair.

I'd noticed that many people whom I now knew by name chatted to me as they came to play against us, but virtually ignored Greta. Even Lily no longer seemed to find as much pleasure in sparring with her. Friends, or rather acquaintances, like Pamela spoke to her only when she spoke to them, which was rare.

At times it did make me feel sorry for her, but almost as soon as I did, as if she could sense it, she'd make some kind of foul remark, which dispersed all my sympathy. Nevertheless I could not help but see her as a lonely old woman. Now that she was no longer as friendly with Sandra, she must be quite alone. Of family, she only ever spoke of a nephew who lived out in New Jersey somewhere. If he himself had any family, she never mentioned them.

Now, tonight, she asked me about my Christmas in Wales, and indeed seemed quite interested.

'I bet your wife was overjoyed to see you.'

'Yes,' I said with a grin, 'she was.'

In return I asked her how she had spent the holidays – 'although I know Christmas is not your festival,' I felt compelled to say before she could. She said she'd been out to New Jersey to see her nephew.

'Is he all the family you have?' I asked.

'More or less', she said, looking uncomfortably about the room for our next opponents. She never tired of blowing her own trumpet but seemed strangely unwilling to talk about herself when asked a direct question. This night however she opened up a little.

'You know, we always wanted to have children, my husband and I. But I had three miscarriages. Then the doctors said I would never have one.'

I told her how sorry I was. It was the first time I'd seen her indulge in anything like self-pity but it didn't last for very long.

'Oh, all that's over and done with now. You can't dwell on the past.'

But her earlier delight was now dispelled. We didn't do very well, not that we did anything particularly bad, but things didn't go our way. A couple of finesses I tried failed. A finesse is when you have a gap in the honours of a suit, and try to work out or guess where the missing honour is, so you can bypass it, as it were. Consider the following hand in Clubs:

```
              North
              A Q J
West K 7 5              East  10 6 4
              South
              9 8 3 2
```

Say you, playing South, were declarer (ie playing the hand). The North hand as dummy would be on the table, and of course East and West would be holding their cards so you couldn't see them. If the lead is in your hand you would play a small Club towards dummy. West, as second player, would normally play low so would put down the five. You would bank on West having the King – sometimes you could have worked it out from the bidding - so would play dummy's Jack. The Jack wins the trick cheaply. You can repeat the manoeuvre next time you have the lead in your hand. If West plays the seven, you can win with the Queen, leaving the Ace to beat the King on the third round (another Bridge maxim is: It's the Ace's job to capture the King). Note that if Clubs are trumps, or you're in No Trump, or all trumps have already been played, or only you and dummy have trumps left, the remaining Club in your hand, however small, becomes the winner. Thus, the humblest card of the pack, the Two of Clubs, can triumph, given the right circumstances.

A few times that night I needed a finesse to work to make the contract. A tenet of bridge play is that if there is only one way to make a contract, you have to give that way a shot, even if it seems unlikely to work. That's what I did, but the odds were stacked against me. The law of averages would suggest that one of the finesses you tried in an evening should work – and there are complicated formulas for working out exactly what the odds are – but none did. Even when you think you know what you're doing, things can go terribly wrong, another of Bridge's lessons on life.

Greta was annoyed, and as usual did not trouble to hide her feelings.

'Well, Mr Second Class,' she said at the end, 'no need to bother to wait for the scores tonight – we're going to be way down. Off you go.'

And with that curt dismissal I was left to make my way back to my tiny apartment, tail between my legs, wondering what lessons the game held as far as partnerships were concerned. At times like this, I could get disheartened about the whole game, about my progress or lack of it, the small defeats obliterating the grander victories. And sometimes it was only Greta's tyranny, and my own perception of her loneliness, that kept me going.

And so my thoughts turned to Ewa. I'd given her a call when I got back into town, and she'd invited me round to a party at her parents' place the next night to celebrate her father's birthday. I wondered if this was wise, considering that last time had had such a negative effect on our relationship. Maybe Ewa was aware of this too and was hoping to redress some kind of balance. The other reason I had cold feet about the party was that I was mulling over the question of whether to leave New York in a few months and go back to Megan. Was it fair on Ewa or indeed her family to string her along? Wouldn't it be kinder and easier to make a clean break now? Somehow I couldn't bring myself to do it.

Naturally I didn't voice any of this, and Ewa sort of assumed I would come. I was to make my own way there, as she would be helping her mother get everything ready. I'd been putting off deciding what, if anything, I'd say about our future. This was not quite how I'd envisaged seeing her again, in a room full of merrymakers. She was so enthusiastic about me going over to Brooklyn that I couldn't refuse.

She greeted me with a warm hug and kiss and a large glass of vodka. She looked glamorous in a black off the shoulder number and that scarlet lipstick she wore for special occasions framed her infectious smile. Things were in full swing when I got there, full of relations, workmates, friends, neighbours. This time there was a definite Polish flavour to the fare: smoked hocks of wild boar, kabanos sausages and pickles, preserved mushrooms, kluski noodles and delicious dumplings called periogi.

Her family seemed pleased and not a little surprised to see me there, I thought. Maybe it was unusual for Ewa to bring a man home a second time, for her family to see her so relaxed and at ease. I was treated like one of their own and the contrast with Greta's sterile world struck me even more forcibly than before. I determined to sweep aside any qualms I'd had about the evening and enter into the spirit of things.

One thing led to another and Ewa and I ended up staying in one of the guest rooms at the top of that huge old house. When I woke up and gathered my bearings, I was alone in the bed. I opened the blinds and the sun was fairly high in the sky. I shuffled downstairs in that hungover, tentative way of emerging late into a quiet house after a party.

Ewa and her mother were sitting at the kitchen table, drinking coffee, the debris of breakfast scattered around them as others had left and gone about their business. They were chatting quietly and contentedly, but stopped when I appeared at the door. Her mother made to get up from her seat when she saw me.

'Come on in, Al. Now, what can I get you?'

'No, you stop where you are,' I said, gesturing with my hand. 'Coffee will do me. I never eat breakfast.'

'Well, that'll never do. Let me fix you some eggs, at least. How'd you like them?' Ewa merely smiled.

'No really, I couldn't eat it.' I poured myself some coffee from the brown enamel jug on the stove and joined them at the large table, covered in oilcloth. Maria pushed a basket of English muffins wrapped in a cloth towards me. I obliged. They were still warm.

'And how's the head this morning?' asked Maria.

'As well as can be expected, I suppose.'

'There are enough sore ones around here this morning, the Lord only knows,' she said with a chuckle. 'It was such a lovely evening. Thank you so much for coming and keeping Ewa company. I know she finds us a little trying at times.' She patted her daughter's hand.

Ewa looked annoyed at this, and as soon as I'd finished my coffee she announced she had to go back into town and asked if I was coming with her.

'They really like you,' said Ewa in the subway train.

'Well, I really like them,' I said brightly.

'No, I mean they *really* like you,' she stressed. 'I can't tell you how wonderful it is to be able to take someone home and relax. My family and friends don't usually get on too well.'

'Perhaps it's something to do with my ability to swig back vats of vodka,' I said.

'Perhaps,' she said pointedly, with a smile. She mocked the way I said perhaps, which to her sounded formal and old-fashioned, rather than maybe. We were getting on - some of the old awkwardness between us seemed to have disappeared, strangely. Yet I felt uneasy, worried that I was being drawn closer into her life and family at the very time when I knew my own path was now heading in a different direction.

She had to work that afternoon but the next day we went boating on the lake in Central Park, something I'd long wanted to do. It was a misty day, and there weren't many boats out, so we had fun exploring every little inlet and cove. Ewa wanted a go at rowing too, and as we were trailing along an elderly guy in a baseball cap passed near us and shouted, 'Now, what's wrong with that picture?' with that jovial familiarity that New Yorkers have, despite their reputation for rudeness. Ewa scowled at him and smiled back at me, and again I felt a pang of guilt at deceiving her somehow.

I played with Marco at the New Cavendish the next Tuesday. We did OK. We went for a few beers afterwards in a bar on Amsterdam that Marco knew. This was his neighbourhood, and he nodded to the bartender and some of the guys nursing drinks at the bar. I had late classes on Wednesdays and Marco, as a freelance journalist, seemed to do as he pleased. In the past I'd tried to find out what stories he was doing, and for whom, but he was evasive. Whether this was because he was working on something big and couldn't say, or something small and didn't want to say, I couldn't tell.

I soon got round to telling him all about Megan and Ewa. I suppose I found it easy to talk to him because he didn't say much, but having listened he would give firm, clear opinions which helped me sort out my own feelings whether or not I agreed with him.

'So that's my dilemma,' I said. 'I want to go back to Megan in the summer and now Ewa wants to get closer.'

'But what is this dilemma, exactly?' he drawled, eyeing up a woman sitting along the bar from us. 'Have fun with Ewa while you can and then it's sayonara and back to Wifey.' It was his familiar mantra.

'But I think Ewa wants to take it a stage further. I don't want to lead her on. Or her family, for that matter.'

'Ohhh, you're not leading her anywhere,' he said impatiently. 'You're both grown-ups and it's only a commitment if both of you want to commit. Keep 'em guessing.'

'It sounds so straightforward when you say it.'

'That's because it is, you baciagaloop.'

'Bodge…a..?'

'Baciagaloop. It's a word my grandfather uses. He's Italian. It means jerk. Putz. Nincompoop, I suppose you British would say.'

'Anyway, we're always talking about my love life. What about yours?'

He took a swig of his Michelob. 'Oh, I do OK.'

'Are you doing OK now?'

'Oh yes, I'd say I'm doing OK now,' and gave a little smile and wave to the woman along the bar.

Sometimes, just sometimes, I wished I could be more like Marco.

Chapter Twelve

Megan and I began quite a regular exchange of emails, mainly about how her illness was going. For me it was easier this way, without any awkward pauses or fumbling for words in a phone call. Perhaps she'd have liked me to phone now and again, but didn't say anything so neither did I. One step at a time, I suppose.

She had a lumpectomy at the Heath Hospital at the end of January. She wrote that it all went off as well as it could have done, and they didn't find anything more sinister. She said she felt OK, not too disfigured. The relief put a bounce into my step. All thoughts of the other Megan, the Megan who dumped me and hurt me and whom I didn't recognise, were now fading fast. She didn't mention returns, or dates, or promises. That was another trait I'd always admired in Megan, she knew how to handle men – me in particular. Because she stayed silent on the subject of our getting back together, I wanted it more and more.

Ewa these days was more relaxed than ever, so of course was more attractive, more fun to be with. I wondered if there was anything in

Marco's tenet that women are keener if you play a close hand. I couldn't let this go on with Ewa, however, and decided I had to take matters in hand, to say something to her.

She'd got tickets one Monday evening for a performance of Monteverdi's Vespers at St Patrick's Cathedral. She liked that kind of thing. It always surprised me that she took Catholicism quite seriously, if not at all assiduously. It surprised me because she'd rejected so much of her upbringing, was a true Bohemian in most ways. I'd asked her once, early on in our relationship when the question wasn't so dangerous, if she thought she'd ever get married.

'What, and be a drudge like my mother?' she said. 'Just running around after men my whole life?'

There was a lecture before the concert about religious music in Venice in Monteverdi's day – well, I suppose most music was religious then. Singers used to be dotted around the catwalks above the congregation of St Mark's, so that the sounds came from all directions, high and low. This format was adopted for the concert, and I pondered how awesome it would be when there was no electronic entertainment or light. The one soprano had a terrific voice – clear, pure and strong – and when we came out I was so filled with a kind of spirituality I rarely experienced that I wanted to savour the moment, not to sour it.

We ate in a little Italian nearby that Ewa knew: spaghetti, meatballs and cheap red wine. I didn't like it very much. It was too bright and because there were so many tiles – even on the tables – it was noisy, echoey, like a canteen. It didn't make my task any easier. Thinking back, as I was, I supposed I'd always been vague with her about my long term plans, partly because I was so vague about them myself. I was still torn between speaking up and letting things ride for a while. But in my heart of hearts I knew it was time to tell her that I'd be going home in the summer.

So without really knowing how I was going to go about it, I tried to slip it into the conversation nonchalantly, as I thought Marco would have done. Ewa was telling me about the latest research she'd being doing in Harlem.

'I've been enjoying my time at Stuyvesant,' I said, and thought I detected a slight pause as she carried a forkful of meatballs to her mouth. 'But I don't think my year will be extended.' Her face and fork fell.

'So what will you do then?'

'Go back, I suppose.'

'Go back?'

'Back to Wales.'

'When?'

'In the summer.'

'Why?'

'Well, my visa only lets me do the work I do now, at the faculty.'

'Well, what about,' she thought for a moment, 'us?' We hadn't spoken about us for quite a while.

'Uh, I don't know. We'll have to wait and see, I guess.'

'That's not very gallant. Couldn't you try to get another exchange, or whatever?'

'Hmm, I suppose I could look into it.'

I could tell she was angry and upset, and I couldn't blame her. I'd handled it badly, I knew. After that neither of us could get out of the place quick enough. Outside I thanked her for a lovely evening, let her make the running. She said goodnight with a weak smile. I wanted to hug her but thought it would come across as a tacky gesture. We didn't make any arrangements to meet up. She was taking the V train back to Chelsea, I was taking the 4. I was feeling low in the subway. The passengers in the train around me all seemed tired and miserable too.

Greta was in one of her friendlier moods around this time. Friendlier to me at any rate. Opponents got it in the neck as much as ever. The next Friday she told one man off for running his finger through his hair, and a poor woman she should lose weight if she was ever to move quickly enough from table to table.

Before the game started, she'd asked me up to her apartment the next evening for what she called pick-ups. I took these to be canapés. She never seemed to imagine I'd have any other plans. I hadn't heard from Ewa in the week, and was wondering what the weekend would have in store for us. But I gave in to Greta.

'Sure. Thanks.' It was pointless trying to refuse her – she'd get her way in the end.

'And I've got something to ask you – your opinion.' Well, this was a first. 'It's about my girl.' Her girl, I knew, was her cleaning woman from Ecuador who didn't speak much English. Some money, around a hundred bucks she thought, had gone missing. She'd left it out on a shelf in the kitchen ready to pay some bills. She wanted to know if she should confront her with it.

'But why do you think it was she who took it?'

'Who else could it have been?'

'Don't you have any visitors?'

As soon as I asked it I thought this question was a little tactless.

'No-one came into that apartment between the time I put it there and the time it disappeared except her,' she stated firmly.

'But you could have mislaid it. It could still be there behind a jar of coffee or something.'

'It's not.'

'Maybe you only thought you put it there – could that be it?'

'No.'

'Well, what about the super – doesn't he have keys?'

'It wouldn't be him, he's been there for years. Longer than I have.'

'Have you spoken to her about it at all?'

'I couldn't do that.'

'Well, I'd suggest you just say something to her offhand, not confront her or accuse her. Just mention you've mislaid some money and ask her if she's seen any bills. See what her reaction is – give her a chance to sort of find it for you, if she did in fact take it. You'll probably be able to judge her sincerity. But you can't do anything without some kind of evidence....'

I was interrupted by the arrival of our next opponents, Lily and 'that woman who drinks.'

'How's it hanging, big boy?' asked Lily with a wink as she took her seat in what must have been a calculated move to antagonise Greta. It succeeded. Greta glowered at her. She usually refused to acknowledge any vulgarity, as she would have termed it. Lily took no notice, clearly enjoying herself. She and her partner were the two people at the club I got on best with, apart from Marco, and the conversation flowed between the three of us. I liked the fact that the college professor got on so well with the dance teacher. Greta was ignored and she clearly hated it. She was reduced to barking barbed comments from the sidelines, and wasted no opportunity in treating Lily with the utmost contempt and downright rudeness. I knew I would pay for this fraternising with the enemy.

Greta had quite a nasty cough that night, but when the professor coughed once, she told her she should leave the table if she was going to cough all over it. The professor looked appalled, and Greta promptly went into a coughing spasm herself.

'You should take something for that,' I said to her.

'Like arsenic,' Lily said to me in a stage whisper.

The professor giggled.

When we'd played our last hand she looked at me coldly and said, 'Thank you for advice about the missing money.'

I could tell she was unconvinced. She had that hard glint in her eyes. 'I'll see you tomorrow,' she said and, in a highly unusual move, got up and left before the results were posted.

I didn't hear from Ewa the next day and didn't call her. I got to Greta's apartment at six sharp, as instructed, dragging my heels a little and not looking forward to the evening ahead. The pick-ups were arranged on her huge glass coffee table, a real feast. There were little French toasts with boiled quail's eggs and caviar, circles of anchovies with capers, mini latkes, knishes and truffles. She served me a delicious Chablis from the crystal decanter with the silver stopper. I was handed a little white plate with one of her blue lace napkins.

'Come on, eat. Don't stand on ceremony,' she ordered. So there was to be just the two of us. I was surprised, and a little discomfited. Greta herself ate next to nothing, but seemed to enjoy watching me make a pig of myself. It was all so appetising. She did enjoy entertaining, you had to hand that to her. Nothing was too good for her guests.

She asked after my wife, as she usually did, and this time I could answer with sincerity that I was missing her and looking forward to seeing her again. I didn't mention Megan's illness. We talked about people at the club, but I soon got fed up as she put each one down one by one with some curt, caustic comment.

'Did you think about what I said about your cleaner?' I asked, wanting to change the subject.

'Oh, I let her go,' she said with a wave of her hand. She was already swept aside, forgotten. I hate that American euphemism at the best of times, as if the employer is carrying out an act of kindness, like freeing a caged bird. But I was shocked at the terrible swiftness of her autocracy. She must have told her that very day. Again I couldn't help suspecting Greta of some ulterior motive. It was odd that she should ask my advice, for the first time, and then so quickly do exactly the opposite. Could it be that she was punishing me for chatting to Lily last night? I'm not usually given to such conspiracy theories but there was something about Greta that drove you to it.

'Why, did she confess or something?'

'She didn't have to. I knew she'd taken the money. I just told her I wouldn't be needing her anymore.'

That was Greta all over. Just when you thought you'd finally put a finger on that one ounce of human kindness, she'd reveal her true colours. I knew that she was fond of her girl, as she called her. But people came and went in Greta's life, and went pretty quickly most of the time. I could understand why. I was inordinately angry for some reason. Marco was right. Why bother with her? I saw her now as a dour dowager, a rich bitch with no regard whatever for the lives or feelings of others, with not one redeeming quality. Not one feature, as you'd say in Bridge. It reminded me of what you're looking for when you open three of a suit, in what's known as a pre-emptive bid. It means you don't have enough points to make a normal opening of one of a suit, but have six to eleven points and seven cards in one suit, let's say diamonds. Odds are that your partner will have at least one or two diamonds, so that should be trumps – there's no point in looking for a fit in another suit. Opener has very little in the outside suits, but if his hand is this unbalanced, other hands may well be unbalanced as well, so there should be opportunities for trumping. The aim of the bid is to get straight to the point, cut out the opposition from the bidding, and keep the contract as low as possible. Partner should only reply if he has opening points and a so-called feature in another suit, meaning a good crop of honours, usually three court cards. If you have no feature, you should pass.

In Greta's case, she should pass. No feature worth mentioning. Maybe this was what she *was* doing in life. Passing. Contenting herself with her Bridge. Not making any promises to anybody. Expecting none back.

After this the conversation become strained. Greta herself seemed to have lost interest in the evening. I made my excuses and left. When I got in the lift there was an elderly woman, the collar of a lilac maid's uniform peeping out over her overcoat. She looked exhausted, worn down, but she managed a weak smile.

'Good evening,' she said, with a slight nod of her head, in that formal, old-fashioned way of the Caribbean - Jamaican I would say from her accent.

'Good evening,' I responded. 'How are you?'

'I'm blessed, thank you,' - again with that weak smile and nod.

What a fine answer, I thought. I imagined her long trek home to a small flat in Queens, having to cook a late supper for her husband after a long day slaving away, skivvying for some upstairs aristocrat who might one day let her go on little more than a whim..... And she could still count her blessings.

My attitude towards Greta changed after that. I felt less sorry for her, less protective towards her. But it was hard to stay angry with her for long. On Valentine's Day a few days later she sent me a card, one of her own cards embossed with her name on the front. A pink crepe paper heart was stuck on the inside. Underneath she'd written in her spidery hand, 'From your partner and friend, All my love, Greta'.

I thought it odd, but it fitted in with my picture of the batty, lonely old woman, and it brought a smile to my face. I put it on the bookcase and thought little more about it. It was the only one I had. I wasn't expecting one from Ewa and hadn't sent one, but wondered if she'd call. She hadn't by early evening, so I called her. She was predictably cool, and I found myself being equally cool in return. I asked when she wanted to meet up. Maybe in a day or too, she said. How about Friday? She knew that was Bridge night. Was she testing me out? Or signalling that she couldn't really be bothered to remember my routine? I suggested Saturday evening instead, promised to cook. She accepted.

I decided to cook something typically Welsh, and spent the day looking for the right ingredients for leek and potato soup, and lamb stew, or cawl as it's called in Wales. I quite enjoyed it when I got into it, got some good wine and candles. I asked myself if this was going overboard, setting a romantic scene when I should be letting her down gently, as it were. But I wanted to do this for her.

When Ewa arrived she looked with approval at the small kitchen table set out with the wine, candles and paper napkins.

'Have a glass of wine,' I said, 'it won't be long'.

I was just ladling out the soup when I heard her exclaim, 'What's this?'

She was standing by the bookshelves, turning over Greta's card.

'Well, I guess it's a sort of Valentine card.'

'I can see that.'

'From Greta, my Bridge partner.'

'Hmm – how old did you say she was?'

'Seventy-seven if she's a day.'

'Don't you think it's pretty weird for her to send you a card like this? Cut out the heart with her own liver-spotted hands, by the looks of things.'

'Mmm, I did think it was pretty weird.'

'Maybe it's time I met this Bridge partner of yours.' I couldn't tell if she was teasing me or not.

'Are you getting jealous?' I asked, putting my arm around her shoulders.

'No, I believe I'm questioning your honesty.'

'Are you serious?'

'Yes I am. I'd like to meet her.'

It was impossible for Greta and Ewa to meet, of course. As far as Greta was concerned I'd been happily married to Megan all this time.

'But all we do is play Bridge.'

'That's not true. You go to her apartment.'

'Yes, I've been there a couple of times for something to eat.'

'Why wasn't I invited? Does she even know about me?'

'Uh, I can't really remember. We mostly discuss Bridge'.

This was turning into our first real row. I thought she was being very unreasonable, all of a sudden. It was very unlike her. But she wouldn't let go of it.

'Look, since when couldn't we have our independence? That's what we both wanted, wasn't it? I don't expect to see all your friends.'

'I thought things were moving on from there. I thought you'd realise that when you met my family for the second time. But obviously that meant nothing to you.'

'Aw, come on Ewa. You're being ridiculous'

'I'm being fucking ridiculous, am I? Let me show you ridiculous,' and she stormed out, leaving me to console myself with wine, soup and stew.

She called me a couple of days later and, very unusually for her, suggested we meet in a bar she knew I liked between our apartments, in Union Square, in an hour or so. Neither of us offered an apology. On my way there I wondered if she wanted to give one, or receive one. But when I saw her ordering a drink at the bar she was all smiles. She ordered one for me and ushered us to a table. She seemed to have put the other evening behind us. I couldn't make my mind up whether to mention it or not – probably not, I decided. I was still in a dither about how to handle my return, what to say to her without explaining everything, which I couldn't. I'd grown so fond of her, and undoubtedly we had clicked, but could just as easily unclick.

I was mulling all this over while she was making small talk, reviewing her week, or the last days since I saw her, as she liked to do. I felt that warm, comfortable easiness I felt with her more and more. She looked at ease too, drinking back her vodka with abandon.

'Al, I have something to tell you. I like you a lot, more than I have anyone for a long, long time. I've so enjoyed the times we've had together. And it's true, I've come to rely on you more and more, without really wanting to. But I think both of us, hand on heart, would say that it isn't going anywhere, that it cannot be.'

I felt compelled at that point to try to interrupt, but she ploughed straight on.

'And I want to be honest with you. There's someone else I like and who I'd like to see more of. He seems to take it more seriously than you do. So I don't think we should see each other again.'

Chapter Thirteen

It was the ideal solution to my dilemma in a way. Everyone should have been happy. Yet I couldn't help feeling aggrieved. I hadn't seen it coming (I'm clearly not very good at seeing things coming) and even thought for a moment it might be a ploy, to test me. But it wasn't. She looked happy, resolute. And somewhere deep down I was glad about that. But my pride was hurt, and I couldn't figure out why she'd done such a complete volte face. Not so long ago she was talking about our future. She obviously hadn't liked me talking about going back to Wales, had wanted me to show more commitment to her. I wondered what Someone Else had that I didn't. US citizenship, perhaps. I felt like protesting that we should carry on seeing each other. But I didn't. So Ewa walked out of my life with a kiss, a smile, and not a backward glance. I thought I'd never see her again.

I can't deny I was bereft. Apart from anything else, she'd been a good companion, something of a soul mate in this vast, mad city. She'd shown me parts of it I wouldn't otherwise have seen. Through her I'd come to understand better the city and its people, its past. She'd made me more curious about the past too. This wasn't much of a consolation, right now, though. Some of those old feelings of emptiness, pointlessness came flooding back.

So I stayed at the bar in the restaurant and made a night of it. Got talking to a group of boisterous office workers. The British accent came in handy in New York sometimes, and it provided them with a couple of hours' entertainment. They tried out their favourite Britishisms on me in ridiculous Dick Van Dyke cockney accents and seemed to find it hilarious as Americans often do.

'Good day Guvnah! Fancy a lift to the Elephant and Castle?'

'Or how about a couple of pints and fish and chips in the pub?'

It was a momentary distraction.

Soon after that Megan and I began to phone each other. With Ewa out of the picture, I think I may have made the first call. Megan seemed more emotional after her operation, even though it had gone well and the signs were good. I needed her too. I began to talk about getting back together in the summer. There was no little doubt in my mind that that's what I now wanted to do, despite everything. We agreed I'd go back for the Easter vacation and stay at my parents. But we'd see a lot of each other, see how it went.

I emailed my counterpart Tyler in Cardiff to see how he was getting on. He seemed to be enjoying himself. I told him I had to come back for personal reasons. He'd think it over and let me know. Then I went to see Vanessa. She said I'd been doing good work, the students were engaged and the classes were getting good feedback. I got the impression I could stay longer if I wanted to. I told her I'd been in touch with Tyler and he was thinking about his next steps. I wanted to leave the door open though, and asked Vanessa if there may be future opportunities at Stuyvesant for exchanges, or research or whatever. She said they could certainly consider the possibility.

About a week later I heard from Tyler, and he said he'd decided to come back to New York. I informed Vanessa about our decision. The New York experiment now had an air of finality about it, as if I was marking time. I lived on automatic pilot, just thinking ahead to Easter. I continued to play Bridge on Fridays, and Tuesdays if Marco had nothing better to do. It was the highlight of my week in many ways.

Since that episode at Greta's apartment I'd cooled towards her. I was perfectly polite but didn't feel the need to look out for her quite so much. Greta of course didn't notice, or affected not to. There were no further invitations to her home, though. Up till then it had been at the back of my mind to invite her out for a meal – I couldn't quite see her huddled round my kitchen dinette. Now I no longer worried about it. I'd see out my time here, turn up dutifully on Friday evenings. I no longer cared that she was alone, and would be even more so when I'd left. She deserved to be.

The flight from JFK at Easter already had an air of routine about it. Like last time, Dad was at the station to meet me, looking as he usually did. On the way home he gave me tidbits of family news and gossip in his un-newsy and un-gossipy way. I told him I was going to see Megan, without mentioning her illness or the fact that I'd seen her at Christmas.

'Well, all the best to both of you,' was all he said. I'd taken the day flight this time, so it was very late when I got home. Mam was waiting up, like she always used to when I lived with them, but I was exhausted and went straight to bed.

I slept in late the next day, after a vivid dream that I often have, or at least think I do – it's hard to tell. This one was so real that within it I woke up and realised I had been dreaming, only to experience the same thing again, so kept telling myself that this time it was for real. I'd moved to a new house, or sort of flat. Megan was there vaguely in the background, only sometimes in was Ewa, and even for one nightmarish second, seemed to be Greta. The new place was dilapidated, almost a ruin, but had lots of potential and was supposed to be bigger than the small flat we were living in but I couldn't quite see how it could be. It was a mysterious house, and when I came to explore it one or two of the rooms were sort of large cubbyholes hidden behind small doors, dark and full of rubble. I kept looking around for the potential, for the supposed extra space. I began to wonder if I'd made a mistake.

The dream was both uplifting and disturbing at the same time. Its significance didn't escape me: the desire to move onto something newer, better, no matter how comfortable you are where you are. I wondered what had brought it on: my return from New York, or Megan's strike for freedom in the first place. Or could it have been sparked off by coming back to my parents' place again, thinking back to when I left, remembering my awkwardness coming back to stay last time?

When I got up Mam was ready to cook me a full breakfast. I could tell she wanted to, as her way of welcoming me home, doing something for me, so I couldn't refuse, even though I had long got used to making do with coffee and a bit of toast or something like that.

She sat down and watched me eat. Dad must have been pottering in the garden somewhere. She was obviously enjoying watching me wolfing it all up. I was hungrier than I thought – long flights and different time zones always seemed to throw my stomach into a state of confusion. Her eyes were sparkling over the rim of her tea mug. Part of me wanted to push her away, as I had for a while when I was a teenager. She seemed a little nervous. Perhaps she too was remembering times when I told her not to interfere. I could see she was plucking up courage to say something. Dad had probably told her about Megan, although I wished he'd waited for me to tell her, and I wished she could wait until I was ready to tell her.

'Don't mind me for asking, but Dad says you're going to see Megan.'

'Yes, Mam, I'll see her tonight.'

'Well, I don't want to be pushing my nose in where it's not wanted. But best of luck to the both of you. You know we all think the world of her.'

'Yes, Mam, I do know.' I thought maybe I should tell her that we were thinking about getting back together. But no, one step at a time.

'Be sure to give her our love, won't you Al?'

'Yes, Mam, I will. And don't worry – your nose is never out of place.'

Megan and I had agreed to meet in a bar in the Bay that we used to know. It was one step further from that new place in Canton we tried at Christmas, and even quite near to our favourite restaurant where she'd dumped me over a year ago. The Bay had changed again, even in that space of time, I thought. Boardwalks were humming with people, families, gangs of exuberant boys and girls. It was now completely unrecognisable from my student days, when I suppose we got a certain thrill from slumming it with the down-at-heel, seedy dregs of the community, the leftovers from the heyday of Tiger Bay.

When Megan came in my first impression was that she'd lost some of that hauteur that I'd once prized and then despised. She almost ran into my arms, right there by the bar, like some terrible TV ad. I didn't know whether to be glad or sad. Not sad at seeing her again, but about losing some part of her that I cherished. But all such thoughts were lost in that first embrace. I could feel tears on my neck. When we eventually broke free of each other I half expected a crowd to have circled us and be applauding, cheering. Of course they were all too busy jostling for position at the bar to notice anything at all.

We sat down and things tumbled out hurriedly and higgledy-piggledy: reaffirmations of love, promises of new beginnings, sexual endearments. We got up and walked back along the Bay to our old house on the Esplanade. On the way back she apologised over and over again. I asked her to stop.

'You just don't know what it's like to lose some of the trust of someone you love,' she said. 'It's like when they tell you in a fire drill to evacuate the building straightaway without picking anything up at all. Just save yourself and make for the stairs. Whereas we all think in reality we'd try to grab just one or two precious things.'

'So why didn't you grab me?'

'You're not really getting it. There wasn't a building on fire when I dumped you. I was snug, smug, but wanted new horizons. I thought you had them more than me. You'd mentioned the New York exchange but never really discussed it, consulted me. Oh, I know you thought you did. But you more or less assumed I'd go along with what you wanted, come with you, or wait here for you. Illness does that for you, though. Focuses. Now I know the first thing I'd grab would be you.' She shouted out the you, over the wind coming in from the sea, in a way that I had to believe.

We ran up to the old marital bed, nervous like teenagers, giggling even, not really knowing what to do, how to place our hands, yet wanting desperately to please, trying to work out if there were new boundaries, if we had to work up to things slowly.

We woke up happy but unsatisfied as well, I think, and ready for more, like newlyweds. I rang home and said I was with Megan, and wouldn't be coming back tonight.

But Mam had news of her own.

'Your Dad's gone,' she said. I knew immediately what she meant.

'But he seemed fine yesterday,' I said, rather pointlessly.

'He just went in his sleep,' she said. 'It's how the doctor said it would be.'

'How are you?'

'As well as can be expected, I suppose. It's a shock of course. But he wouldn't have wanted to be an invalid. And neither would I.'

I dashed straight up, of course. Kath was already there. Mam was down to earth, busying herself with practicalities.

'Do you want to go up to see him?' she asked.

I didn't particularly, but thought I should.

He looked peaceful, younger, as if he were merely having a Sunday afternoon nap. I spoke a few inane words and kissed him on the forehead. I was glad that I'd come to say goodbye.

Neighbours came with food, to pay their last respects and see if there was anything they could do. After everyone had gone I sat in the kitchen with Mam over a cup of tea.

'What now for you?' I asked.

'Well, I'm not going to sit by the fire in black like my granny did,' she said after a moment's thought. 'I'd quite like to do some travelling. Your Dad was never that keen, and towards the end had got a bit set in his ways, it has to be said.'

Dad had stipulated in his will that there should be no tears at this funeral, and that there would be money behind the bar at The Malsters for a good drink afterwards.

So it was quite a jovial affair in some ways, with his cousins from the Rhondda and some of Mam's relatives from Mid-Wales. She'd got the Treorchy Male Voice choir to come and sing his favourite hymn, *Arglwydd Dyma Fi (Lord, Here I Am)*. It was quite a squeeze in the small chapel at Glyntaff Crematorium. Megan was at my side.

We took Dad at his word and had a good drink after the service. The Rhondda lot loved a good funeral and we ended up doing the Hokey Cokey.

And so it was back to New York for the final haul, as I'd begun to think of. To Greta I simply said that I was going back to Wales for a while, but would probably be back. She looked displeased, offended.

'I don't want you to go,' she said, peering over her cards as if I was doing something deliberately to upset her.

'I'll write to you,' I promised rashly. 'And I'll be back before too long - you'll see. She was not mollified. She was curt to me for the rest of the evening, and rude to everyone else.

'Stop spitting,' she commanded one poor old guy who nervously spluttered out his bid in the face of her hostility. 'And you must use your bidding cards instead of your voice.'

As so many opponents had done before him, he gave her a quick, uncomprehending glance and looked around the rest of us in turn in a kind of appeal. Had we witnessed it? What should he do? I gave him a weak smile of empathy, sending him telepathic messages: 'She's like that to everybody. It's not you. There's nothing to be done. Just carry on.'

The summer term dragged on. And then one Friday afternoon I bumped into Ewa in the courtyard outside the Stuyvesant library. She was looking good. She asked me if I had time for a coffee. I couldn't think of an excuse quickly enough so we strolled over to the cafe on the other side, ordered lattes and sat outside. We made small talk, catching up. It was all very relaxed, but I could tell she had something to say and was building up to it. I wanted her to get it over with.

'So how's the new relationship working out?' I asked eventually.

'It isn't,' she said. 'He was a charmer who couldn't keep his dick inside his pants.' She'd obviously been hurt, again by someone else who couldn't keep his dick in his pants. Each relationship seemed to confirm her view of men in the image of her philandering father. Except, I couldn't help reasoning with myself, I hadn't cheated on her. Or had I, with Megan, from the start?

'I'm glad I bumped into you again. In fact I've been working up to giving you a call. I was wondering if we could try to make another go of it?'

I had no idea how to handle this. Whatever I said, I'd end up feeling in the wrong.

'But I'm going back to Wales before long,' I said. 'Back to my wife.'

'Oh,' she said, and looked crestfallen. I suddenly wanted to reach out and rub her shoulder.

'I'm sorry. Perhaps I shouldn't have said that.' I think I had told her I'd been married ages ago, but made it sound as if it was in the past. At the time it probably was.

'No, no - I'm good,' she said. 'You can say whatever you like. I'm fine.'

We sat there in silence for a moment or two.

'Maybe we could meet up for a drink before you go,' she said, looking out into the courtyard at the passers-by. I knew I had to answer straightaway, not be seen to weigh things up.

'That'd be great,' I said. 'I'm going to be a bit busy but I'll look in my diary and give you a call.' That came out all wrong. But she didn't seem to notice.

'Promise?' she said, looking back at me now.

'Promise,' I said.

When we parted she kissed me on the cheek.

I'd been seeing quite a bit of Marco. For all his apparent popularity, especially with women, he spent a lot of time on his own. I suspected I was something of a back-up, to be rung in the evening if nothing or no-one else had turned up. Not that I minded. He'd served my purposes too. He'd been a good pal in a way, and although it was hard to get close to him, he'd been my kind of touchstone these last few months in New York. I often found myself wondering What would Marco do? What would Marco say? But our friendship never went beyond Bridge or bars. I couldn't imagine going to see a play with him, or an exhibition, or even a film. But then I never asked him. He probably thought the same about me.

When I turned up at the Bridge Club for the last Friday before I was due to leave, Greta was sitting holding court to her disgruntled courtiers even more stiffly than usual. She didn't look around or even up as I approached, but waited for me to sit down and come into her eye level, like a headmistress, or someone interviewing you for a job.

'I've been to the hospital today,' she opened. She pressed her thumb between her index and forefinger, making a sound with her tongue like a ratchet. This was her mime for the injections she had now and again. I assumed they were for her back and neck, to help that stiffness of hers. She'd tell me about her hospital visits, her shots, but unusually for an old person, I thought, refused to go into detail, even when I asked.

'It's not pretty,' she would reprimand. 'You don't want to know.'

'It seems to be getting worse,' she said this time, 'and the shots more and more useless.'

I wondered idly if this final mention of her weakened condition was a tactic to keep the attention focused on her, rather than talk about my plans for departure, and future plans. If so, it worked. I was very solicitous that last evening.

I don't think we went out with a bang exactly – must have come fifth or sixth. I escorted her down to her car in the basement.

'You've been like a son to me,' she said finally as she put on her gloves before she got in the car. I opened the door for her, and she heaved herself in. 'I don't know what I'll do without you,' she said, and it sounded like an accusation.

'Well, you've got the New Cavendish, haven't you?'

She made a sound like 'Harrumph.' 'I don't know for how much longer. Clarke has been complaining about the rent. He says they might have to move.'

'And you've got your new cleaner.'

'Oh, yes, my Irish girl. She's nice. Lovely brogue.'

Her Irish girl was the hit of the moment. I wondered how long that would last.

'And your nephew comes to see you from time to time.'

'Oh, well yes, he's my beneficiary..........'

There was no consoling her, I could tell. There were to be no cheery goodbyes.

'Well, I'll write.'

'Yes, do that. Send me picture postcards once in a while from your travels.'

She always stuck to her belief that I travelled a lot in my job – I'd given up trying to dissuade her – and seemed to like to think of us as both world travellers.

'And keep up the Bridge. There's no reason why you shouldn't do well if you persist. After all, you've had an excellent teacher.' There was no smile on her face. 'And give up those cigarettes. You don't need me to tell you how bad they are.'

'I keep telling myself, but myself doesn't listen.'

I heaved the door shut, and she set off at her stately pace, peering over the dashboard, not looking back. I remember thinking, 'I won't see her again,' and not particularly caring.

I spent the next couple of days packing the few belongings I was taking back. The rest of the stuff I was giving to the mother of one of my students who'd just arrived penniless from Kosovo. I'd got talking to the student and she mentioned her mother was coming over with just one suitcase – her house had been destroyed. I explained I was leaving for Wales and she'd be welcome to the bits and pieces I was leaving behind. I just said it for something to say really, some way of showing support, but the student jumped at it, so we had to make the arrangements to have them picked up. When I thought about it I didn't have much worth giving, and felt a bit of a heel using charity to offload my unwanted stuff.

They came around on the Saturday morning before I left on the Sunday evening – the student, her mother and an uncle with a U-Haul. The mother was tiny and unsurprisingly looked sad, and embarrassed. She'd baked me a cake.

As it turned out, when I saw it all being moved out, I realised that I'd accumulated quite a bit in that small space in that small amount of time – it's amazing what you can: a sofabed, bedding, desk, lamps, plants, crockery, pots and pans.

When it was all loaded up and the uncle was making sure it was all secure in the truck, the mother began to cry. She spoke to her daughter with little sobs. The daughter turned to me and said her mother wanted to tell me something.

'She just wants you to know how grateful she is for all of this. She's never had to accept charity before in her life.'

The mother blubbered and jabbered on, wiping her eyes but keeping them on me. She grasped my hand.

'She wants you to know she had a lovely home in Kosovo,' continued the dry-eyed daughter in an oddly monotonous, dispassionate, translator's tone. 'She never thought it would come to this. You're doing a great thing. It will come back to you.'

The mother and I hugged, and that almost set me off as well. I didn't know whether to feel less of a heel or more of one. After they'd gone the little place was echoey, soulless, as if my presence in the city was already being eradicated. I felt as if I were just one more nameless person of the hundreds and thousands who came and went unremarked. I couldn't help giving it a lingering, nostalgic look. I was due to spend my last night on Marco's sofa, after a few beers no doubt. In the past few days I'd thought more than once about giving Ewa a call for that farewell drink, but somehow just hadn't got around to it. I regretted it now, but it was too late. I made up my mind to write to her when I got back.

On the subway I continued my reflections on my year in New York. I was certainly in a much better state than I was the year before. And in so many ways, I wouldn't have missed it for the world. That's what you say, isn't it? Except that I would have missed it, if Megan hadn't dumped me in the first place. But you can't think like that, can you?

My stay had taught me to see America and Americans with different eyes, in large part thanks to Ewa, but Greta and Marco and all the others too. I'd also thought a lot more about Europe and the Europeans in the days of vast immigration – why they left, what they felt as they did, what kind of life they were hoping for when they arrived. And it wasn't so long ago, within the last hundred years for many of them, within the memory of people I have known. Persecution, poverty, hunger, war. It was the first time I'd ever really thought of life like that, so near. And it was going on now, in modern Europe, in the Balkans. I thought of the woman from Kosovo and her life in a suitcase.

When I got to Marco's apartment there was a yellow post-it stuck on his door.

'Al, old chap, sorry and all that, but I've been called out of town on a job. Should be back later this evening. The super will let you in. Ground floor #1G.'

All of a sudden I felt all alone and depressed at the prospect of an evening by myself in Marco's flat. I went downstairs to IG and found the super in. He was a large man with a paunch and the kind of moustache that seemed part of a super's uniform. He seemed to be expecting me. I asked if I could leave my bags at Marco's and then I had to pop out for a while.

'Sure thing,' he said, automatically. 'As long as it's not too late.'

I went outside and found a phone booth. I dialled Ewa's number, confident that she wouldn't be in, or that she'd be busy that evening. Well, at least I'd have kept my promise and tried. But the receiver was picked up after four rings.

'Hello, Al,' she said brightly. 'I'd almost given up on you.'

'I've just been a bit busy with everything,' I said. 'You're not free tonight by any chance, are you?' It's my last night in New York.'

She was. I suggested we meet in the Old Town Bar, and got the B train down to 23rd Street. I grabbed a beer at the bar and settled down to a wait, but Ewa was at my shoulder before I knew it. She looked great.

We had burgers and beers in one of the booths. She seemed to have decided to overlook the fact that I'd left it so late to call her, or at least made no mention of it. In fact we were both relaxed and natural, the mood of those first few carefree weeks we'd been unable to recapture after things seemed to get more complicated. We opened up to each other. I told her she'd meant so much to me, that she'd made my time here so wonderful. She in her turn said when she found herself getting fond of me she began to worry that she'd be hurt again – she hated herself for it but couldn't help it.

'I kept telling myself to trust you, but somehow I couldn't. It was a vicious circle. The more I got to like you it seemed the more jealous I got. Jealousy and mistrust are terrible things.'

'Well, I wasn't exactly open with you,' I said. 'I was still terribly cut up about Megan, and I wasn't myself, but I couldn't tell you how much I wanted her back.'

'Why not?' she asked simply.

'I was afraid it would put you off.'

We both laughed at how stupid we'd been. And now, with our hair down at last, the hours flew by. Before we knew it, it was eleven thirty. If Marco wasn't back it would be too late to bother the super. One thing led to another, and I found myself walking back with Ewa to her place, and staying the night. We both let ourselves go more than we ever had done, and it was wonderful. It was as if this was what we'd be looking for all along, to lose ourselves in each other, and never quite managed it.

When I woke, I rang Marco's to check that he was back. I could tell I'd woken him up as he gave one-syllable answers, but he'd be around until later that day. Ewa was still sleeping. I debated for a while whether to wake her, but decided not to. Apart from anything I couldn't face the farewells. I would miss her a great deal and wanted to go before I changed my mind.

I found a pad and pencil by the phone and wrote her a note which I hoped came over as warmly and as genuinely as I felt towards her. I gave her my parents' address as somewhere she could reach me. For a minute or two I watched her face. I wanted to lean down and kiss it. She stirred slightly. I couldn't risk it. I let myself out and made my way up to Marco's.

Chapter Fourteen

It was a year and a half before I went to New York again. Megan and I had decided on a long weekend before Christmas. There had never been a word from Ewa. Marco and I would exchange an email from time to time. I'd kept in touch with Greta, sent her postcards from holidays and breaks in Europe, given her the odd phone call. I thought she sounded slightly frailer each time, her voice losing some of that stentorian authority. She in her turn sent me Christmas cards, or at least those printed cards with her name on the front wishing me Happy Holidays, and occasionally a scrawled note with print-outs of her Bridge scores when she came top, I noticed, as if to show that her brain was as good as ever and that she was getting along without me very well. I also saw that she rarely played with the same person twice. Sandra's name appeared next to hers, but not very often.

Two weeks before we left for New York I gave her a call, saying I'd be in town for a few days and would love to see her. Her voice sounded diminished, somehow, with a new note of self-pity.

'Oh, I don't know about that. I don't get out as much as I used to, or entertain,' she said.

'Greta, I just want to see you for a few minutes. To find out how you're doing. You needn't go to any fuss at all.'

'You might get a little shock to see how I'm doing,' she said mysteriously. 'Give me a call when you're in town,' and promptly hung up.

I'd also tried Marco, but he was out of town for the duration. I'd have liked to have seen Ewa, but couldn't think of an easy way to do this. We were going Christmas shopping, Megan and I. It was our Christmas present to each other – the last trip we might take for a while because Megan was pregnant. We'd booked into a cheap and cheerful hotel in the East Village, a sort of Bohemian chic place with shared bathrooms. It was said Madonna had done a photo shoot by a water tower on its roof. But the fact that it was so inexpensive meant we needn't stint on the little luxuries like a cab into the city from JFK, rather than the hours it would take on the subway.

The cab driver was a chatty Trinidadian called Mohammed. He recognised our accents as British and when we told him we were from Wales he was even chattier, declaring there was a special bond between Trinidad and Wales. Our accents sounded familiar to each other, he said. Mohammed said he loved Christmas.

'Forgive me for mentioning it, Mohammed,' I said, feeling like old friends now, 'but Christmas isn't exactly your festival, is it?'

'Oh, I'm from Trinidad,' he laughed. 'We love all the festivals there. We celebrate them all – just another excuse for limin'. Eid, Dawali, but particularly Christmas. You should come down and see. We love all the carols, the black Santas, even fake snow in the shop windows.'

What a civilised approach, I thought. It's odd that for such a Christmassy city as New York people could now scarcely bring themselves to say the word. I told him that I'd worked at Stuyvesant University and they'd stopped having Christmas parties and went for the Miami beach one in an effort not to offend anyone.

'Madness, man,' said Mohammed, shaking his head. 'PC gone mad.'

I couldn't help agreeing with him. Often when you heard the phrase 'PC gone mad' it was from the lips of some bigot objecting to some kind of progress. But, as unchristian as I was, I still felt it wrong that people couldn't celebrate Christmas if they wanted to. It came to me that I'd missed the melting-pot aspect of New York in all its glorious diversity more than I'd thought. Cardiff is quite cosmopolitan these days, but not quite the world-in-a-city that New York or London is, and far from the old Tiger Bay, crossroads of the Seven Seas days.

Manhattan did indeed look Christmassy as we sped over the Queensboro Bridge and down 2nd Ave. I felt an old rush of excitement and could tell Megan was loving it too. We were like two schoolkids on a Christmas outing. Megan had wanted to do all the festive things – we booked in to see the Christmas spectacular at Radio City, we'd go shopping at Macy's, skating at the Rockefeller Center, and to a carol service at St John the Divine. There were certain sights though that brought back the times I had with Ewa. It was as though I was aware of her shadow disappearing round a corner, her laugh being carried away by the wind, always just out of reach. I tried to put her out of my mind, to concentrate on enjoying myself with Megan, but her ghost kept popping up at the most inconvenient of times.

We'd both agreed it would better if Megan didn't come to see Greta, if indeed she was going to grant me an audience. I'd told Megan all about her and she was intrigued, kept asking questions.

I rang Greta the next day. 'Well, I'm here,' I announced to a distinctly lukewarm reception. 'Could I maybe call in to see you on Sunday afternoon for a few minutes?'

'Well, I suppose so, but I won't be able to do much for you.'

'I don't want you to do anything, just a quick chat.'

'Very well. Be here at three-thirty. But you'll have to leave by four-thirty.' Click.

'Perhaps she doesn't want you to see how frail she's got,' said Megan when I told her about it.

'Mmm, maybe,' I murmured, although couldn't quite see Greta foregoing an attentive audience under any circumstances.

I got to her apartment block about fifteen minutes early, as nervous as a naughty schoolboy outside the headmaster's office, and paced up and down outside smoking a couple of cigarettes until it was time for my allotted hour.

I had to announce myself to the uniformed concierge, who seemed to look me up on some kind of list.

'OK, you know where to go?'

I said I did, but then realised I wasn't sure any more, and he must have seen a hesitation. 'Tenth floor, door opposite the elevator.'

I rang her bell and waited for what seemed like several minutes. For a moment I thought she'd changed her mind and decided not to see me after all. But then the door opened slowly and there stood Greta in a Zimmer frame.

'Bet you didn't expect to see me like this,' she challenged. In fact she didn't look as bad as I was expecting – it was only now I saw her that I recognised that I'd prepared myself for a marked deterioration. Her hair was completely white, and her face had that grey pallor of pain; she was a little heavier, puffier and a little more hunched, but it was the same Greta – not a hair out of place.

'Go ahead and sit down. I'll have to shuffle on behind you.'

The place was as spotless as I remembered. I could see the vacuum swirls in on the plush cream carpet. I wondered how she managed it.

'Do you still have your Irish woman?' I asked, sinking into the sofa.

She looked at me for a moment as if she didn't know what I was talking about.

'I have three different girls,' she said, clearly satisfied with the arrangement. 'My Tuesday girl, my Friday girl, and my Sunday girl.' Even her cleaners have to spread the load, I thought.

'Here, I've brought you something,' and handed over a package of the perfume I remembered she'd asked me to get that Christmas. She opened it slowly, and when she realised what it was plonked it down on her lap with a sigh and a shake of her head as if to say, 'You shouldn't have.' I could tell she was touched though, and I was pleased.

'So how are you doing?'

'Oh, don't ask. The brain's alright. I don't go to the New Cavendish any more. There's a little group of ladies here in the building who get together now and again. I think they're thankful to have someone of my calibre play with them. But it's the body, the body that lets you down.'

She spent quite a while listing her many ailments. It was clear she was often in pain, found it difficult to get going in the morning.

'This will happen to you, you know,' she warned, jabbing her finger in my direction in that old familiar gesture. 'You young people think it will never happen to you, but it will. There's no fighting it. Your body gives up in the end. It creeps up on you. However....,' (she always had a distinctive way of saying the word, like two separate words with heavy emphasis on the second syllable: How. EVah), 'at least the brain is working. And it's the brain that counts, you know. I read the obituaries in the New York Times. It's not the athletes and keep-fitters who live the longest. It's people who use their brains, who are creative. Scientists, conductors. That's where Bridge comes in.'

With one of her rare questions to me, she asked if I'd kept up the game. I started to tell her that I now played in a club in Cardiff with Megan, that we even took part in tournaments and did quite well, but she interrupted me – I was only allotted a certain amount of time. 'Well, you had a good teacher.'

But she wasn't finished with her long litany of complaints. There were renovations to the building which were costing her an arm and a leg. 'I couldn't get into a retirement home because I'm too over-qualified.'

'Over-qualified? How?'

Greta rubbed her thumb and forefinger together.

'You've got too much money?'

She nodded.

'I worked hard all my life, day and night. My husband and I ran a large business, you know. I saved for a rainy day. Well, now it's raining.'

'How's Sandra?' I asked, running out of appropriate sympathetic noises to make.

'Oh, Sandra died,' said Greta impatiently.

I was shocked and sad to hear this news, particularly delivered in such a dismissive way. I'd always liked Sandra, and admired the way she stood by Greta but stood up to her too –would only take so much of her nonsense.

'Well, I tried to tell her but she wouldn't listen. She had some bad symptoms, swollen feet and whatnot, and I told her to go to the doctor. But she didn't of course. She wouldn't listen to me. She only had herself to blame.'

This set Greta off on another train of thought.

'She was always coming round here. I didn't mind. I quite liked doing things for her. But you know, she never asked me to her home once.' She thought about it for a moment. 'Maybe she thought her home was not up to my standard. People worry about that kind of thing, don't they? She needn't have. I would have understood.'

I was aware that by now my time was almost up, and I was glad for it. I'd had enough. I got up to make a move, but Greta stopped me.

'Before you go, I've prepared some afternoon tea. That's what you English like isn't it?'

'Welsh,' I corrected, my heart sinking slightly at the prospect of sitting through yet more of her gripes and groans.

'Ah yes, of course. Do you Welsh like tea too?'

'Oh yes, we like tea,' although I hardly drank the stuff myself.

I helped her out of her chair and we shuffled into the dining room. It was all laid out on a white cloth, with those dainty blue lace placemats and coasters. She had me make the tea and bring out a Stollen cake and some soured cream that was put out in the kitchen.

'I thought this would be nice and Christmassy for you. They used to serve this in the Old Country.'

I was then charged with finding a butter knife in the cutlery drawer. I had no idea what a butter knife looked like, so pounced on a fairly odd looking one and held it up quizzically.

'No, no, that's a fish knife,' she said with a certain glee, clearly enjoying my helplessness, in the way old ladies do with young men.

I found the right knife and sat down to tea. I couldn't help thinking what an odd picture we made, the two of us.

'You spoil me, Greta.'

'Oh, I can't help it. I'm like that. But I don't entertain much these days. I wasn't going to see anyone today but you were so persistent.'

'Greta – I made two phone calls,' I protested. Surely even she couldn't imagine I'd badgered her into seeing me.

The coquettishness was back.

'I was such a party girl. Always having people around, always entertaining. I was an excellent cook. Our business partners used to remark on it.' I'd heard all this before but there was no stopping her. 'We travelled everywhere, like you do. I've been everywhere. Germany several times.' She gave me a piercing look. 'People hate them, but there's good and bad in all of us. I've met some real nice ones. But I've also met some bastards,' and she delicately popped a small slice of cream-smothered Stollen in her mouth and licked her fingers. The phone rang.

'Would you get that for me please?'

I don't know what made me do it but when I picked up the phone I put on the voice of a very correct English butler and said, 'Greta Heller's residence.'

There was silence for a moment. Then a spookily familiar voice enquired, 'Is this the right number for Greta Heller?'

'Uh, yes. Who shall I say is calling?'

'It's her sister.'

I almost dropped the receiver. In all the time I'd known Greta, she'd never once mentioned she had a sister. As far as I knew the only family she had was the nephew out in New Jersey somewhere.

'Greta, it's your sister,' I called out.

'Tell her I'll call her back,' came the immediate reply.

'She'll call you back.'

'At her convenience,' snapped the sister, sounding exactly like You-know-who. She even hung up like her.

'I didn't know you had a sister,' I said as I sat back down, looking forward to this story at least.

'I don't speak to her,' she said, munching contentedly.

'Why not?'

She looked at me indignantly. 'What do I want to listen to all her trials and tribulations for?' she demanded. I thought this was a bit rich, even for her, given that she'd spent the last hour or two detailing all hers to me.

'What's her name?'

'Bathsheva,' she said, dismissively.

I wanted to know about her, about the rift between them, but Greta wasn't forthcoming. I managed to get out of her the fact that she also lived out in New Jersey, in a large house – I think ranch was the word she used – but not much more. So the sister sat in her mansion in the countryside while a few miles away Greta sat alone in her smart apartment. There was something terribly sad about it.

'Does your nephew still come to see you?'

'Oh yes, he comes,' she said, as though she wished he wouldn't.

I glanced at my watch. I'd been here more than two hours. Megan would be waiting for me back at the hotel. But Greta didn't seem to want to let me go. She resorted to asking me what I was doing with my time. 'Still wandering about all over the place?'

'I'm thinking about doing some writing.'

'What will you write about? Bridge?'

'Hmmm....maybe.'

'Well, don't forget your teacher's name.' She spelled out her middle name for me, an unusual one. I wondered for a moment if she was joking, but then remembered she didn't have much of a sense of humour.

'I'll look forward to reading it, if I'm still around.'

I looked around the lovely room, and tried to see it through her eyes: a lifetime's collection of mementos and memories, the record of a life. I wondered what would happen to it all when she was gone. Her nephew wouldn't want a lot of it, I decided. His home would be full of his own things. A wife, probably, but no children. I saw him in a Trilby hat with thick black-rimmed glasses, a pipe, and driving gloves.

At last I managed to take my leave. 'You were a good Maitre D,' she said, refusing to let me do the washing up. Her girl would put it in the dishwasher.

'And we were a good team. Always on top.'

I forgave her this indulgence. I forgave her lots of things.

When I got back to the hotel on East 17th Street, Megan was waiting, eager to hear how it all went. We went to a little diner we'd taken a fancy to on the corner. Our room was so basic we couldn't stay in it for very long – a double bed, two hard chairs, one bedside table, a washstand and a shop-style clothes rack on wheels in an alcove in the corner.

Megan was full of questions, so I related some of the self-centred, one-sided conversation.

'You should write this down,' she advised.

'I do write it down, some of it.'

'She sounds awful. Did you find the One Good Thing?'

'No, it just seems to get worse. Her sister rang and she wouldn't talk to her, and when she told me her best and probably only friend had died, she seemed more annoyed that anything else. I think she's a lost cause. I'll have to give Marco his hundred bucks.'

Megan told me not to throw in the towel just yet. She seemed as intrigued as I used to be by Greta. Maybe I'd discover something when I was least expecting it. Or maybe not. I was losing patience and interest in her.

Chapter Fifteen

Six more months passed. The cards and calls between me and Greta dwindled. I tried to give her a ring once in a while to check on her, but didn't do it as often as I should have done. When I did she sounded more or less the same: told me all her aches and pains, took a lot of medication I think, no longer went out.

I'd kept in touch with Tyler, the guy I did the exchange at Stuyvesant with. We'd done a couple of papers together for our respective journals looking at the BBC and PBS and public radio in the USA and now there was the possibility of a book about media in the two countries. He asked me to go over for a couple of days to talk to his publisher. I decided this time to go alone – Megan was looking after our daughter Beth – and stay on Marco's couch.

There was quite a bit to arrange with Tyler beforehand and, what with one thing and another I didn't get round to ringing Greta till a couple of days before I left. After that last time I was nervous about asking myself round, let alone actually going to see her. But when I did ring I got her voicemail and left a brief message saying I was going to be in town and would call in to see her if I had time.

The weather in New York was blisteringly hot. It couldn't have been more different from last time. Marco's minute apartment was like an oven, and the clunky old air conditioning unit in his window above the sofa seemed to do nothing other than keep me awake at night, but it was unbearable when I turned it off.

Not that we spent much time there. Marco and I caught up on things in some of the neighbourhood bars we used to hang out in – quite a novelty for me now, since the birth of Beth. He told me that the New Cavendish had moved down to Chelsea. The landlords raised the rent and they had to find somewhere cheaper. Many older players couldn't make it down there, so membership had fallen off and it wasn't the same. For some reason this came as quite a blow to me. How could they do this behind my back, I wondered unreasonably. At least Greta never saw it, I reflected. Somehow I could not picture her in bohemian Chelsea, even if she could get down there. I was grateful that she would remember the New Cavendish in its heyday, in her heyday.

'You gonna look up your old dame?' asked Marco as we sat in the Old Town Bar. It was as if he was reading my thoughts.

'Yeah, I was thinking of dropping by,' I said, with a little snort of a laugh – self-deprecating, I suppose.

'Found that one redeeming feature about her yet?'

'No, and I don't think I ever will. Which reminds me.....'

I fished in my pocket and made to hand over four twenty dollar bills and two tens. Marco waved it aside.

'Come on,' I said. 'A bet's a bet. I insist.'

'Tell you what. Give me half now and half when she goes. It can't be that long now.' He snatched the bills and swaggered over to the bar, shouting over his shoulder. 'Oh well, it'll all go down the hatch anyway.'

I was to meet Tyler next morning at ten-thirty in his office – my old one. I was somewhat worse for wear, no longer used to drinking as I used to be. It was odd being back at the university, all the more so because classes had finished for the summer, so the place had an abandoned but also anticipatory air, as if someone was watching you from the seemingly empty halls. And in the baking heat, I almost expected to see tumbleweed roll across the central piazza.

Most of my students would have graduated by now, and once again I had that feeling of being left behind, as if the scenery had changed behind my back, as if I no longer knew the plot.

I had a good meeting with Tyler though. He'd already been talking to the university press and things were looking promising for our book. They just wanted us to flesh out the outline a little more before meeting with them the following day, so we spent a couple of hours doing that.

We went to lunch in the cafeteria, which ran a limited service in the summer for the members of the academic staff who still came in to do some work and people attending the various conferences they held in the summer months. I was somehow nervous about seeing Ewa there, even though I knew she too must have left by now. I had no idea what I'd say to her if I did. I was half hopeful, half expectant, half fearful. That's too many halves but you know what I mean. I didn't regret that last night I spent with her and, after what Megan had done to me, was determined not to feel any guilt. I was glad it hadn't been left at that night when she walked out on me in that Italian restaurant. But our last night together felt more like a beginning than an ending. It felt like how it should have been all along. I often thought about her, what she'd be doing, who she was with.

That afternoon I went down to Greta's apartment. The doorman was there in his heavy coat and high hat. I marvelled how he could wear them and stay so cool. The sweat was dripping off me, wearing just an open-neck shirt.

'I'm here to see Greta Heller,' I announced.

'Is she expecting you?' he asked, eyeing me suspiciously.

'Sort of. She knows I'm in town, and I told her I'd call round to see her.' He gave a little snort as if to say Well, that won't get you very far.

'Have a seat,' he said, nodding at one of the huge sofas. 'I'll call up,' and he lifted the receiver on the phone on his desk. There was a short, muted conversation. I couldn't make it out as he'd turned to face the front door. He put the phone down and beckoned me over.

'I'm sorry, she can't see you today,' he said, with something approaching pleasure.

'But I'm leaving the day after tomorrow for the UK.'

'I'm sorry,' he said, ushering me out of the building. 'Not today.'

'Couldn't I just talk to her on the phone?'

'I'm afraid not.'

'Well, could you just tell me if she's doing OK?'

He paused a moment, deciding whether to say something or just walk back into the building.

'She's doing OK, I guess,' he said gruffly. 'Getting older like the rest of us.'

'She's being looked after?'

'She has everything she needs.'

Maybe not everything, I thought on the subway back up to Marco's. But I wasn't quite beaten yet. I rang the next evening, and was a little surprised when I heard the phone being picked up, and the familiar voice announced, 'Greta Heller'.

'Greta,' I said, 'it's good to hear you,' and meant it, if only because I didn't like failing. 'I've been trying to see you. I called round yesterday afternoon.'

'Well, you have to give me more notice than that,' she said belligerently. 'You can't expect just to walk in here and I drop everything.'

'I just wanted to see how you were doing,' I said, already exasperated. But Greta was in no mood for small talk.

'How do you expect me to be doing? I'm getting by.'

'Well, I'm going back tomorrow but the next time I'm in town I'll let you know well in advance.'

'That would be a very good idea.' Click.

I was furious now, and sensed there wouldn't be a next time. I was angry that she hadn't even mentioned our daughter. I'd written and sent a photo when she was born. She could have just asked after her, thanked me for the picture, no matter how ill she was. She could talk, couldn't she? A final slap in the face from Mrs No Good Thing.

I was still angry with her three months later when I got an email from Marco saying he'd heard Greta had died. I can't say I was surprised, or even very upset, but I did mourn her passing. She was a one-off.

'I guess that's that,' wrote Marco. 'You'd better wire me over those fifty bucks.'

Somewhat callous, I thought, although no worse than Greta deserved. Would anyone mourn her?

Megan had a similar reaction.

'It's a pity you'll never get to know her secret', she said, 'or even if she had one'.

But I wasn't ready to quit quite yet, and emailed back to Marco saying he'd have to wait a little longer while I made some enquiries. It was as though, if it was not too late, I wanted to begin the quest for her One Good Thing in earnest. Privately though, I had no idea what enquiries I could make, or of whom.

I knew only the sister's first name, and she was bound to have a different surname. The nephew's name I had never heard at all, and as these two were the only family she'd ever mentioned, he was bound to be the sister's son, so he would have a different surname too. Mind you, she hadn't told me about her sister until that day she telephoned. Maybe there were other relations she never spoke about, or to. But even if there were, how on earth could I find them?

I didn't even know what temple she went to. I had the impression it was fairly near her apartment block. She didn't seem to stray very far from home. Her apartment block! I had the address. I could maybe start there. I got the general number from International Directory Enquiries – I'd only had Greta's direct line - and rang it. I'm sure it was the same surly doorman who answered.

'Uh, hello, my name's Al Evans. I don't know if you remember me,' – slight pause, no response – 'but I used to visit Greta Heller from time to time.'

'She passed away.'

'Yes, I heard that. I'm just trying to contact her family. Would you be able to help?'

'I'm afraid not.'

'Could you tell me which synagogue she went to, then? I'm pretty sure it must have been in the neighbourhood somewhere.'

'No, I'm afraid not.'

'Could you give me any information at all about her?'

'No, Sir, I can't help you.'

'Do you know anyone that can – neighbours, her cleaners?'

'No, Sir.'

Bastard. I'm sure he must have known something that could have helped me. I went back to the synagogue idea. At that time I'd just began googling on the internet – a friend had told me about it – so looked up synagogues in the Upper East Side. There were about a dozen which sounded plausible. I set about ringing them one by one when I had a moment, late in the evening. I must have gone through six or seven before I got anywhere. I managed to speak to the Rabbi and asked him if he knew Greta Heller.

'Yes, I do think I recall that name,' he said. But he couldn't really help me very much. He was fairly new there – had arrived a couple of years before when the old Rabbi died. He could remember Greta coming in the first few months. She didn't mix much, didn't participate in the social life around the synagogue. She'd been buried out in New Jersey somewhere, he didn't know where exactly. I asked him if any of the congregation (is that what it's called in a synagogue?) would remember her. He said he very much doubted it, but he'd ask around a little and let me know. At least he'd tried to be helpful, and had given me his time. I left him my email address and waited for a couple of weeks, but nothing came.

I began to get dispirited by it all. How quickly the traces of a life can disappear. I almost let it go then, as a hopeless cause. But one night when I was googling something else, I got onto it again – I couldn't let it go now.

I remembered how she used to go on about the business she had with her husband – furniture stores as I recalled – the business that had taken them around the world and led to so much entertaining on Greta's part. If it was such an empire, there must have been some kind of record. Maybe that was her One Good Thing, her redeeming feature – the jobs they provided through their own hard work – although it was a bit of a stretch and I had to admit to myself it was easier to picture Greta in the role of slave-driver. I googled 'Heller furniture Manhattan.' I was getting more adept at it now. Nothing.

Then I remembered how she liked the obituaries in the New York Times. Maybe if the business was such a success she'd have got a mention. Not a thing that I could find.

Then all of a sudden it came to me. The Bridge Club! Why hadn't I thought of it before? I'd lost the old number – it had probably changed when they moved anyway – so did a search on bridge clubs in Manhattan. There were quite a few, but as I scrolled down, lo and behold, there it was: The New Cavendish, West 23rd Street. It had changed location but not name. I looked at my watch. It was eleven-thirty – six-thirty in New York - and Clarke would have just arrived for the evening session.

I dialled the number, my heart pounding somewhat by now. I couldn't have told you why. Clarke answered. It was good to hear him, and he spent some time chatting even though I knew it was a busy time for him. So I came to the matter in hand.

'I was sorry to hear about Greta,' I said.

'Greta? Oh yes, you two were quite a team, weren't you?'

I said we'd kept in touch and wanted to track down her family, maybe visit the grave if I was in town.

'Gee, Al, uh, I'd like to help you, I really would, but I don't think I can. The place isn't really the same now, you know. A lot of the old-timers fell off when we moved. It's quite a schlep down here for them. It's just a small club now.'

'Isn't there anyone left who might have known her?'

'Uh, well, you knew Greta. Better than most.'

'She didn't get very close to people, huh?'

'No she didn't. At least, not for very long.'

I felt defeated, as if my last chance had just slipped through my grasp. So near and yet so far.

'Well, thank you Clarke. Good to talk to you again. Bye now.'

'Likewise. And Al.....?'

'Yes?'

'Be sure to come see us the next time you're in town.'

What a nice guy. But he was my one remaining hope. Now I had no more ideas of who to turn to next. Maybe Marco would have, but I couldn't involve him. He wouldn't help me win his money anyway.

I think I had more or less given up when the letter came. It looked rather intriguing, lying there on the doormat among all the bills and junk. It was one of those creamy, parchment type affairs, embossed in black with the name of what looked like a law firm in Manhattan. It was a letter from Greta's lawyers. It said, in dry, high-toned legal language, that she'd willed me her diaries.

Chapter Sixteen

The letter said they could arrange to have the diaries sent over to England, as they put it, or I could pick them up if I was going to be in New York. As luck would have it, I'd been talking to Tyler about meeting with the publishers again soon – they were almost ready to sign a deal. I checked with Megan to see if it would be OK to go over there for two or three days.

'Of course,' she said. 'The diaries might finally unlock her secret.'

I hadn't thought of it in those terms, but when she said that a strange thrill of excitement tingled my back. It was an odd thing for her to do, leave me her diaries, come to think of it. Could it be that she wanted to tell me something, something that was inside those diaries?

I called Tyler and he thought it would be a good idea to meet the publishers in about a month – we should be ready to sign by then.

I emailed Marco to see if he could put me up then. At least it wouldn't be so stifling this time. I couldn't help gloating a little over this latest development.

'BTW,' I wrote, 'Greta left me her diaries in her will. I'll pick them up when I'm over. Get your greenbacks ready. All will be revealed.'

I wrote to the law firm to say I could collect the diaries, and gave them the dates. It was just a couple of weeks later that one of those embossed cream envelopes dropped onto the doormat – I'd been almost counting the days. It was getting nearer to my trip and I wanted to get things fixed up. The letter inside said that her nephew had her diaries, a Mr Arnold Goldfarb of Morristown, New Jersey. They gave a phone number, which I rang at eleven o'clock that same evening. After just a couple of rings a man's voice answered.

'Arnold Goldfarb.'

'Hello, Mr Goldfarb. It's Al Evans here, calling from the UK. I was your aunt's Bridge partner. I'm sorry for your loss.'

'Thank you,' he said, a little impatiently, I thought. 'I suppose you're calling about the diaries.' I told him I'd be in New York for two or three days and could collect them.

'Well, I'm out in New Jersey, you know.'

'I could come out there, if that's alright with you. You can take a train, can't you?'

'From Penn Station to Morristown. They run pretty regularly. If you call ahead to tell me when you're due I'll come bring them to the railroad station.'

'Well, that's very kind of you. Mr Goldfarb – do you think it would be OK for me to visit her grave?'

There was a silence.

'Perhaps it's a little presumptuous of me to ask. We played Bridge quite often together and we kept in touch. I just assumed she would be buried somewhere near you.'

He'd had time to consider. 'I would think that would be in order.'

And so I set off on this rather improbable mission. Megan came to Cardiff Central with Beth and waved me goodbye and good luck. In the train and the plane I guess I should have been concentrating on the book Tyler and I were working on but I couldn't get those diaries out of my head. I'd racked my brains but couldn't imagine what she'd have put in them, and above all why she should have wanted me to have them.

It was good to see Marco again: the same old debonair dishevelment, the same old natty nonchalance, the same old apartment, the same old sofa. Only now, in the autumn, the heat had left the city and I didn't have to have that spitting, spiteful, ineffective air conditioning to keep me awake.

I was surprised that even he was intrigued by the diaries: he couldn't help his curiosity seeping through that blasé exterior of his. 'But what kind of diaries are they? How many are there? What would she have written in them?'

I had to chuckle, rather enjoying this unaccustomed inquisition from him.

'You know as much as I do, Marco. We'll just have to wait until tomorrow.'

I'd played out in my mind several times a little movie about collecting the diaries, adding little refinements each time: what they'd look like, where I'd take them to read, what they would in fact contain. It's ridiculous, really, on what little substance our lives and joys can revolve. It might seem somewhat mean, but in that movie there was no shot of Marco. I'd already decided I wanted to read them alone, in my own time.

When I stumbled off the sofa the next morning, with a slight but not unwelcome hangover, I saw that Marco had already left. I staggered over to the fridge and slugged down some fizzy water. Through his wooden blinds I saw it was a cold, clear day, the blue sky highlighting the autumn leaves to perfection. I set out for the 86th St subway station with that all-too-rare sense of adventure, of purpose. I'm sure I must have sat with a little smile on my face as the train rattled down to Penn Station, buried now beneath Madison Square Garden. I couldn't help trying to picture the station as Greta would have known it when she first set foot in New York: a grand neo-classical temple to train travel in its heyday, less than a century since the railroad had united the States into the nation that we think of them today. After the facade was demolished in the 1960s, nothing remained on the street level, and below was a bewildering labyrinth of corridors and escalators.

I found the train to Morristown easily enough though, leaving in ten minutes. I sat on one of the rather worn leather benches in the chunky, clunky, metallic NJTransit train. We clanked out below the rundown Meat District, through the tunnel underneath the Hudson, across the dreary, depressing New Jersey Flatlands with their reedy wastes and petrochemical skyline on the horizon. Eventually we started climbing a little, through the straggling suburbs, until we reached the leafier parts that told you why New Jersey had earned the nickname of the Garden Sate. Morristown Station was an old fashioned affair, 1920s I would say. From the platform I pushed through heavy wooden doors with small, high panes and walked across a marbled hall furnished with huge curvy wooden benches. I pictured Greta walking confidently through here in the 1940s perhaps, wearing a jaunty felt hat and carrying a small boxy parcel for her young nephew who'd be waiting outside with his mother. I gave a quick glance around the ticket hall to see if there was an elderly man obviously waiting for somebody, but I didn't really expect him to be there. I pushed against an outer door.

Right outside I saw a Yank Tank, as they used to be called, one of those huge square cars that make you feel as if you're driving your living room. Now they seemed the exclusive preserve of the elderly, rich and poor, white and black. Inside sat a short man with thick grey hair and black rimmed glasses, wearing one of those sheepskin car coats and tapping the steering wheel with one of those funny holey driving gloves. I knew it was him instantly, and it was only then I realised that I'd formed quite a precise mental image of him, without thinking about it at all, and for once he matched it almost exactly. He was just missing the Trilby.

He was staring steadily ahead of him. I tapped on the window. He wound it down, electronically, still looking ahead.

'Hello, Mr Goldfarb? I'm Al Evans'.

'Get in,' he said, not altering his position. I took an immediate dislike to him. He was surly and drab. He showed no curiosity about me whatsoever.

'We'll go straight to the cemetery,' he said with the monotone of a bored bus driver.

We drove through the town in silence and as we came out of it started up a slight slope. As we rounded a bend I saw a huge stone entrance with black metal gates, and above it gravestones climbing the hill. The car swept through it like it knew its way. The cemetery was one of those sprawling, wooded places with wide avenues to accommodate the cars. He came to a juddering halt half way up the hill.

'Aunt Greta's just there,' he said nodding to the right as if she were expecting me for a picnic. He kept the car running and clearly wasn't going to get out. That really annoyed me, along with his proprietorial 'Aunt'.

I'd come all this way to see her and he couldn't even be bothered to switch off the car.

'Aren't you getting out?' I asked, feeling like making a point.

'I'll wait for you here,' he said, looking up the hill and beginning to tap the steering wheel again.

I got out and walked slowly across the grass path below the row of graves indicated. It was on the brow of the hill, with empty ground above it dotted only here and there with recent tombstones. Below was a beautiful view back towards New York City, with just the ghost of its skyline discernible through the haze. A good place for her eternal rest, I thought. I made my way reverently along the graves. Here they all seemed to be Jewish, with Stars of David and pebbles placed on top in the Jewish style of remembrance.

I found her about the tenth along, a simple red marble affair. A Star of David on top and underneath: Greta Heller 1923-1999. So she was 76 when she died, about 73 when I met her. She was younger than I thought, but always had that air of a bygone age, another world.

'Hello Greta,' I said inwardly, feeling foolish. 'I hope you're in a good place,' even though I'd never had the slightest religious feeling in me. 'And you were right, we were a good team.'

I realised that I hadn't brought anything with me, any flowers. On the top of her grave there was one solitary stone. I wondered who put it there. The unloving, unloved nephew, sitting there with the smoke pouring out of his exhaust? I couldn't quite see it. But who else? I looked around to find a stone of the right size to put on the other side. I found a nice one, smooth and red, which would go with her decor. I didn't know if it was appropriate for a Gentile (if indeed I am – is an atheist a Gentile too?) to put a stone on a Jewess's grave but I did it anyway.

'Goodbye Greta,' the inward voice said, and again I felt foolish. Why all this fuss? I didn't even like her very much. The old cow.

I walked back to the car, its exhaust still dirtying the crisp autumnal air, dreading the journey back with my new-found mutual enemy.

'I'll take you back to the station,' he announced to the road ahead. I was glad. Maybe before I'd met him I'd pictured us sitting on the veranda of his white clapboard house, sipping iced tea, talking about Greta's life years ago. And suddenly, without knowing it, he'd give away her secret. He'd tell me what her life meant.

For a while I joined him in staring wordlessly at the road ahead. But the silence started getting on my nerves.

'So you're her sister's son?' I asked eventually when sheer tedium had overcome reluctance to try to engage him in conversation. For the first time I felt him shoot me a quick glance of curiosity.

'Yes, I'm Bathseva's son.'

'How's she doing?'

'She passed too.'

'My condolences.'

'Thank you.'

The silence was even more unbearable now. Maybe I would find the answer here in this horrible car, on this horrible journey, with this horrible man.

'Was it recent?'

'Three days after Aunt Greta.'

'Did they see each other before they died?'

'No.'

'What did they fall out about?'

Silence.

'Look, I don't mean to pry, but I was fond of your aunt,' and was conscious of the lie so added, 'in a way.'

He thought about it for a moment. 'They hated each other for as long as I can remember.'

'Why?'

'I don't know. Never did. Maybe they didn't either.'

'So how did you get on with her?'

'We never did. We weren't a close family.'

'Did she ever mention me?'

'I told you, we didn't talk much.'

'What did you think of her?'

'Look pal, we're coming to the railroad station. You'll get what you came for. Let's leave it at that.'

For the first time I detected a kind of nastiness underneath his drab exterior. I'd crossed some kind of line. He pulled up abruptly outside the old station, reached over and produced an old battered leather suitcase from the vast back seat.

'Here's what you came for,' he said again, and it crossed my mind that from the way he was behaving you'd think he was handing over the millions I figured he'd be getting, instead of a few old diaries.

'Can I ask you one more question?' I asked before closing the door.

'What?' he snapped, already revving the engine.

'Did you read them?'

'Why the hell would I want to read them? he said, and started moving off with the door still open, in that stately way that Greta used to. I just about managed to get it closed in time.

I've never been so relieved to leave a person in my life. On the train back I clutched the case as if it held my whole future. I was tempted to open it, but couldn't somehow. I thought of Greta. If that curmudgeon was her only familial comfort in her old age, her beneficiary, then she was even worse off than I imagined. I clung on to it on the A train up to Amsterdam Avenue. When I got back into the flat there was a note on the table from Marco: 'I'm out of town for a few days. You'll have to muck along yourself. Enjoy the diaries.'

And it was only then that I thought of the one question I didn't ask Mr Goldfarb: 'Why do you think she left her diaries to me?'

Chapter Seventeen

I resisted the irresistible temptation to open the case until the next morning. As I lay on the sofa, I enjoyed planning where and when I would do the deed. I can't say why I was so pernickety about it. I wanted to be alone, but not in the apartment for some reason. And it can be hard to be alone in New York when you want to be. In the end I settled on Central Park. It would be cold, but I could wrap up well with several layers and a scarf and a hat. I had no idea how long it would take. One of the great, one of the many great things about New York is that you can look like you want and no-one takes a blind bit of notice, especially in the city's humungous lung of Central Park. Everyone understands that you've come there for your own bit of space and what you do in it is no-one else's damn business.

I took it easy, savouring the anticipation. I prepared meticulously, found gloves and a woollen hat in Marco's surprisingly ordered closet. I put on two jumpers under my warm coat – it was as I expected another blue-skied freezer. I put a rug in a backpack and set off with the suitcase, not caring that I looked homeless.

I had breakfast in the corner diner. Eggs sunny side up, home fries, bacon, link sausages and brown toast – I'd got fluent in American breakfast ordering by now. I read the New York Times, paying particular attention to the obits. They seemed to bear out Greta's theory that people who exercised their brains lived longer that those who exercised their bodies – and that was before the fad for brain training. A composer had died at 96, a pioneering surgeon at 88, a baseball player at 72, a boxer at 66.

I picked up some cold cuts, pickles, bread and a bottle of good Chianti for lunch and maybe even dinner from the next deli I came to. I sauntered to the park and found a nice sunny spot on a slope by Belvedere Castle, overlooking the pond. I spread out the rug, stretched out, and opened the suitcase.

It was a jumble of desk diaries, mainly black or blue, the most recent ones with the year on the cover. I rummaged through and picked out 1996, the year I met her, and flicked through it.

The entries were sparse, in that familiar, spidery hand in her purplish ink that gave me quite a jolt when I saw it: a hair appointment here, a Bridge score there, the result of a ball game and occasionally a terse comment on some political event: 'Clinton Re-elected!' I would love to have known what that exclamation mark meant. For all her autocratic bearing, I'd long suspected Greta of being the unlikeliest of Democrats. What a letdown. There was virtually no narrative here, let alone her innermost thoughts and secrets.

I worked out the date we first played together. Nothing. I flicked forward two or three Fridays and found my name. I don't know why I was particularly keen to find it – like being handed some photographs I suppose and being most interested in yourself in them. Yet if there were some meaning in the diaries, some meaning in her willing them to me, then surely it would somehow be linked to me?

'I've started playing with a young Welshman called Al. I've taken him under my wing.' Hmm, some wing.

I found the date we last played together.

'Al told me he's leaving. But he says he's coming back.'

I looked through some older ones, in the 1960s. These pages were busier, but in the same style of simple records. They detailed her dinner parties (when she was a 'party girl') with complete menus, notes of what certain guests did or did not like, flattering comments from them, successes with the furniture store, what had sold well, how the business was thriving. I could only find references to the one store, but I distinctly remember her talking as if they had a whole chain of them throughout New York and beyond. Maybe there'd been a small branch in New Jersey, but I couldn't find mention of it.

There was a lengthy postcard from Venice, describing its sights and smells, the luxury of the hotel they stayed in, a champagne supper on a gondola on the Grand Canal, a visit to a furniture wholesaler and the purchase of some chairs for a valued customer (those Venetian ones in her living room?)

One of the most detailed entries was a three-day trip to a trade fair in Chicago. I got the impression she didn't think much of the city, but even this lacked her trademark catty commentary.

The weeks and months went by in similar vein. I couldn't see much evidence of her vaunted globetrotting ('Oh, we were always going all over the place') apart from Venice and Milan, but this globetrotting was also a fancy she'd accorded to me.

I ploughed on through the 1970s. The dinner parties dwindled. But there was indeed the odd trip abroad – Berlin, Paris, Buenos Aires – usually combined with wholesale furniture shopping. No mention of Vienna, her home city. Nothing about her parents, who I calculated would at that time be quite elderly. I now assumed they were left behind in Vienna when Greta and her sister came to New York. I pictured them alone in an old fashioned house, cluttered with heavy wooden furniture. They'd be anxious about their daughters in America, and, after the Anschluss, their own future. And then, the day of their deportation would have come. There would be no more letters to New York. Greta would not have known what had happened to them.

Then in 1976, after a mention of the bicentennial celebrations in New York, another simple entry; 'My dear husband died.'

Nothing after that for quite a while, but the Bridge gradually got more and more entries until the Friday night routine became a fixture.

I made a few desultory notes, and with the turn of every page still hoped for that epiphanic entry which would reveal some hitherto undisclosed facet of her nature. But there was nothing I could say 'Yes!' to. Her family were mentioned rarely: so far I hadn't seen one reference to her sister. An occasional visit from the nephew was recorded, often with some rather caustic parting shot about what he did or said, or didn't do or didn't say.

I'd spent a good two hours by now, and was frankly bored and disappointed. I broke for lunch, enjoying my picnic and the wine. It was too cold for a snooze, although my cladding had kept the cold largely at bay, so I packed up, and went for a brisk walk through the woods towards the boating lake. I thought for a moment how pleasant it would be to take a boat out and moor it at some shady, far-flung shore but realised I probably had another few hours to go so it would work out very expensive.

I retraced my steps and found my spot again for the afternoon session. I went back and read some of the 1960s more carefully, just to check I hadn't missed anything. I hadn't missed much. So back to the 1950s. More of the same, and not every year was represented. These weren't diaries as such, just a record of social engagements and a business log. I wondered why she'd kept them all, all these years – and again, why give them to me?

Back to the 1940s, when I calculated Greta would have been embarking on her married life. And so, on June 30th, 1943, it said 'MY WEDDING DAY!' in capitals, and with that exclamation mark (surely it meant joy) (or hope) (or fear.....?). She'd only have been twenty or so. Very young by today's standards. But, without her family, in a strange country, who could blame her for looking for a bit of security? I thumbed through the early months of married life, and there was nothing to illuminate that exclamation mark. There was no mention of the miscarriages she told me about, the heartache she must have suffered. This diary was no confidante. But again some years were missing. Could she have edited them out before passing them on to me? But why?

I'd almost given up, when I came across one of the first passages in the 1941 diary that was so different from anything else that I figured it must have some significance. Here it is in full.

"A woman was walking down a little side street off Bleecker St early one winter's evening. She saw what she thought was a tramp, slumped on the sidewalk, surrounded with bags. She was going to pass by but she noticed it was quite a young woman, weeping. She saw that among the old bags was quite a smart purse. This was no tramp. The older woman stopped.

'Are you OK?' she asked

The younger woman looked up, not at the older one, but at the sky. Her eye make-up was smudged.

'Yes, yes.'

'What's wrong?'

'It's my sister.' She started crying again.

'Is she ill?'

'No, no, not really.'

'Where is she?'

'It's OK. Thank you.'

'Is she nearby?'

The younger woman looked down the street. 'Yes.'

'Can you go see her?'

'Yes, I see her.'

The younger woman was at last composing herself.

'What's wrong with her?'

'Nothing. It's nothing really.'

'Can I take you for a cup of coffee or something?'

'No, really, you're very kind.'

For the first time the younger woman looked directly at the older one, smiled and kissed her hand.

'Thank you,' she whispered. The older woman took her handkerchief and handed it to the other. The younger woman wiped away the make-up damage.

'Keep it,' she said. There seemed to be nothing more to say. 'Well, bye. Look after yourself.'

'Bye.'

As she walked away the older woman glanced back and saw the younger one pick herself up, gather up her bags, and walk unsteadily in the other direction."

This brief episode certainly got me fired up again. But what an odd little story, and what was the point of it? At first of course I assumed the older woman was Greta, but as I worked out the years I reasoned that it was far more likely that she was the younger one. So why was the story told from the older woman's perspective? It obviously had a great deal of significance for Greta, but it seemed she wanted to distance herself from it, not admit to her distress. I pondered over and over it, but could make head nor tail of it, and nothing before or after shed any light on the matter.

This dairy was different from all the others – it was leather bound with thick cream pages. The writing was recognisable but not as spidery. It was the same purplish ink.

Eventually I turned back to the fly-leaf. There was an inscription in a younger, firmer hand: 'Greta Weinstock, 166 Bleecker St, New York City, 1939.' The first entry said, 'This fine diary was given to me as a Christmas gift.' The second said, 'Still nothing from Vienna.' That was the only mention I'd seen of anyone back home, the indication of bad news.

The entries were few to begin with. It described her room, on the fourth floor at the back, at the top of the stairs. Half way through the year, it seemed she moved out and got a job in a furniture store. I assumed it was her future husband's store, but could find no confirmation of this.

And that address began to niggle. Wasn't it familiar from somewhere? And then it hit me. Surely that was the address of that hotel I stayed in when I first came to New York – the Wayside Inn, was it, or something like that? The more I thought about it the more convinced I became that I was right. The address was something like 164-168 Bleecker St. It was three old houses knocked into one, as I recalled. That would make 166 the middle house.

I was excited now, sure that I had at last found a clue. I quickly packed everything up and almost ran over to Central Park West. I found a phone booth with directories hanging on those metal hinges. Almost shaking, I looked up The Wayside Inn. There it was. 164-168 Bleecker St. I ran to the 81st Street subway and got the C train down to Washington Square. On the way over I realised I didn't have a plan. Should I book in for the night and have a good nose around? No, I decided. Better to play it straight. Tell them why I wanted to look at that room at the top of the stairs. The Americans are good at something like this.

It was just how I remembered it, all wooden panels, leather chairs and log fires. I asked the clerk at the small reception desk if I could see the manager.

'It's the Manageress,' said the clerk, looking at me over the top of her glasses. I recognised her, but I wasn't sure she did me, although she gave me a friendly smile. 'I'm not sure. She might be busy right now. Could I tell her what it's about?'

'Tell her I'm researching the history of the place,' I said, to cut a long story short. 'It won't take long. And I can wait, if that's OK.'

'Sure,' she said unsurely, and nodded to one of the leather wing chairs next to the fire. But it wasn't long before an elegant young woman in a black suit with swept-back blonde hair came up to me and held out her hand.

'Hello, Mr – Uh?'

'Evans,' I said, getting up.

'Mr Evans. I'm Carla Crane. How can I help you?'

She was looking me up and down. I must have looked a pretty sight with my old coat, woollen hat, rucksack and battered suitcase. But I decided I liked her. She seemed genuine, and I banked on my accent to win her over.

'Well, I don't want to take up too much of your time, but the thing is I've discovered that an old friend of mine who just passed away used to live here. She left me her diaries and describes her room in them. I was just wondering if I could see it?'

'How intriguing,' said Carla with a smile, and I knew it had worked. 'I'd be delighted.'

I described where the room was.

'That would be 48 – no question about it. I'd be happy to show you if it's vacant.'

She glided over to the reception desk and came back with the key on a huge brass plate.

'We're in luck. It's vacant until tomorrow. This way.'

I left my bags with the clerk and we squeezed into the tiny elevator, having to get unnaturally close to Carla Crane. I filled her in, as she did seem genuinely interested.

'She was my Bridge partner – Greta Weinstock was her name when she lived her just before the war. I think she'd just arrived from Europe. Maybe she stayed her for a while until she found somewhere to live.'

The elevator had come to a shuddering, clanging halt and we poured out into a tiny landing with only three doors opening off it. And there, at the end of the stairs, was Room 48. Carla bent down to unlock it. 'These would have been private houses then.'

'So maybe her family lived here?'

Carla opened the door to reveal a tiny room with a small dormer window in the sloping roof.

'These would have been servants' quarters then.'

Servants? Was it possible that Greta started life in America as a maid? I just couldn't picture it. I'd always pictured her arriving in New York in style, on a liner, in furs. I couldn't adjust to seeing her as a refugee with one battered suitcase, like the one I had downstairs, like the one containing the life of the mother from Kosovo.

'Are you sure? Maybe it was another room?'

'They were all servants' rooms on this floor. If she describes the fourth floor at the back of 166, then this is where she was. This one was knocked through into a linen closet, I believe for the bathroom,' and she nodded to a door in the corner of the room.

I asked her if she knew anything about the family who lived here, still struggling to picture Greta carrying freshly laundered linen up to the closet.

'They were an old, wealthy family, I believe. The Carringtons. Well known merchants in the city at the time.'

She thought they sold the place after the war and it was taken over by a law firm until the three houses were knocked through in the 1980s to form the hotel. I asked her if they had any records of the old family and staff.

'I'm afraid not,' said Carla, still wearing a smile but I could tell her patience was wearing a little thin. 'The place was pretty much gutted when it was made into the hotel. Most of the decor isn't original – it was all brought in for the makeover. And I wouldn't have thought the law firm would have kept anything.'

I took one last look around the tiny room, still reeling at the thought of Greta here in the drab wartime decor, possibly sharing with her sister, fetching and carrying for the Carringtons.

I thanked Carla and made my way back to Marco's in the gathering gloom, disappointed that the day hadn't yielded more, but intrigued by this new Greta, arriving in this bewildering city on the eve of war, working her way up from humble beginnings.

I was flying back the next morning on the day flight. Marco was still away on his trip. I left him a note of thanks and added, 'You were right. No saving grace,' and put it under a paperweight on his desk with two crisp twenties and a ten.

Just as I was about to tuck myself up on the sofa, I heard the keys rattling in the front door. Marco strode in and slung a well-worn leather kitbag on the floor.

'I was hoping I'd catch you,' he said, lighting up a cigarette. 'Wrapped up a bit earlier than I thought.'

He went over to his desk and poured himself a stiff shot of Bourbon, then held the bottle up questioningly to me.

I'd have to leave early in the morning and told myself I should really get some sleep, but wanted to tell Marco about the diaries, so against my better judgement I nodded. I sat up and Marco listened patiently while I told him what I'd read. Like me, he was mystified by the passage with the young woman crying.

'It probably was her sister,' he said at length. Maybe they had rowed and Greta was waiting for her round the corner or something. Or maybe Greta read it in the sister's diary and copied it down out of guilt.'

'You think that was the trouble with Greta? Guilt?'

'Well, they say the oppressed are likely to turn into oppressors. She had the double guilt of leaving her family, and surviving.'

'Guilty about leaving her family?'

'Yes. She left Vienna with her sister just before the war, didn't she? Only a few thousand were allowed to leave under some scheme the Brits cooked up with the Nazis called Kindertransport. They needed to have someone to take them in in Britain, or somewhere else to move on to. One suitcase and one knapsack each. Greta's mother was British, wasn't she? That would tie in. Then somehow the relations in Britain got them over to the States.'

'You seem to know a lot about it?'

'I worked on a programme for PBS about it.'

Far from boasting, Marco looked decidedly embarrassed. I'd always imagined him on the sleazier side of journalism. I had no idea that he worked for public broadcasting, and said so.

'Bits and pieces now and again.'

'So you're not quite the hard-boiled hack I'd taken you for.'

'Oh, I don't know about that.'

'So, they felt guilty, these Kindertransport kids?'

'They could never forget the faces of their parents. You can imagine the scene at the railroad station. Obviously the parents thought it was the only way of saving the children. One father sent a letter with his son and daughter, saying 'They shall not live in fear.' One of the people we interviewed vowed he'd always do what he could for asylum seekers, and he made his career as a human rights lawyer. But on the whole the kids lived with guilt for the rest of their lives, because usually their parents died in the camps. One woman told us she'd always felt like a second class survivor compared to those who'd been to the camps. She always wondered if she'd have had the courage to do as her parents had done and send them away. She felt as if her parents had given her life twice.'

I took some of the early diaries with me on the plane and had a more thorough read. Marco's stories had inspired me once again. What was it, what was it I was meant to find? Maybe it was just a record of her Bridge scores. She was always so proud of them, right to the end, and maybe she wanted to pass them on to someone who could remember. Or maybe she did want someone to know that her life had been a struggle, that she wasn't the rich bitch she appeared. She'd worked hard and survived. For Greta was a survivor. And in my quest to find her lifetime's achievement, perhaps I was forgetting that in many lives, survival itself is an achievement.

And then, as I was putting the diaries back in my bag, something fell out of the top one into my lap. Two black and white photos. I pushed my bag back under the seat in front of me with my foot, and settled back to look at the pictures. One of them was of Greta's wedding day in 1943, just her and her husband standing beside her. I would have recognised her anywhere – the same hauteur, the same air of defiance. The groom was tall, older, serious – every inch the business man. Greta was dressed simply, her dress not a white bridal one, but she was carrying flowers and wearing an odd little jewelled headdress that was not quite a hat but more than a tiara.

The other picture was an earlier one, of the same man but a different woman in quite an amorous pose, locking arms and puckering their lips at each other. On the back was written, 'Bathsheva and Michael, 1941.' It was Greta's sister. I could see the likeness.

It was obvious what had happened. Greta had stolen her sister's boyfriend. That would explain the estrangement. Could it also solve the puzzle about that enigmatic entry in 1941, the tale of the woman crying in the street? I thought about it for a while. And it came to me that the young woman was not Greta but Bathsheva, weeping for her lost love, for what her sister had done to her. How Greta came to know about it, I could only imagine. Maybe Bathsheva told her about it, to show what pain had been inflicted. Maybe Greta witnessed the scene herself, from an upstairs window in the house in Bleecker Street. Maybe it was a product of Greta's imagination, of her guilt – an attempt however feeble to consider her sister's feelings.

So that's what this strange bequest was. It was a confession, one she had never made in life and that she couldn't write about. She couldn't have counted on the fact that I would put in the legwork to join the dots, but it was the nearest she could come. It was the last thing I expected. The betrayal, her betrothal, must have come back to haunt her later, when she was alone. No-one apart from Bathsheva knew about it after Greta's husband died at a relatively young age. Not the rest of the family, according to her nephew. She didn't want them to find out. And she couldn't tell anyone. But she couldn't quite let her secret die with her, either. She had the triple guilt of leaving her parents, surviving, and betraying her sister. She'd leave me the diaries, and let fate decide whether or not I made anything of them.

The secret wasn't the good thing about her I'd been hoping to find. It was a bad thing, putting her in an even worse light. But it did go a long way to explain her misanthropy, her nastiness. She couldn't quite look the world in the eye. And despite what she'd done, life hadn't turned out how she'd hoped it would. There were no children, her husband had died young, her sister was estranged, she'd seen off her few remaining friends.

She was left to die alone. Guilt had hardened her, so that even when her sister tried to reach out to her, as she must have been doing in that phone call I took, Greta maintained her solitary position on the moral high ground, even though she had been the wrongdoer.

It was getting dark outside by now, and we were about an hour away from Heathrow. I dozed a little but awoke with a start. It dawned on me with such blinding clarity that at first I thought I must have been dreaming. How could I not have seen it before? It had been staring me in the face all along.

It was me. It was me all along. I was her One Good Thing, the last trick up her sleeve. In a way, she'd changed the course of my life. I'd been in helluva state when I got to New York, and couldn't see how to go on, didn't think I wanted to particularly. She had indeed taken me under her wing in her own way, and out of myself. Without her imperious command, I doubt I'd have stayed the course at the New Cavendish. Those Friday night Bridge sessions had given me back some sense of purpose. Sometimes your saviour comes in the heaviest of disguises, from the unlikeliest source, when you least expect it. And maybe there were other mes too.

I couldn't wait to tell Megan. When I got back to Cardiff late that night, and told her, she cried.

'I just hadn't really realised what I'd put you through,' she said in a weepy whisper. 'I'm so sorry.'

I hadn't thought of it like that, that that was the message she'd take away. It was possibly cruel to have told her, and I said so.

'No, no, I should know,' she said. 'I'd like to have met her.'

'Yeah, she was quite a character. Crusty as old bread of course, but who can blame her?'

I'm writing all this up years later. Megan and I didn't make it after all. We never quite found our balance again. In some ways, she's still the love of my life, but no longer the love *in* my life. What happened had left a permanent crack in our relationship.

The break-up was amicable, and I see a lot of Bethan, who's twelve. I still play Bridge, both at the club in Cardiff where I can now hold my own with Scary Mary, and what we call kitchen Bridge with some old friends. A couple of them have been going through pretty rough patches recently – relationships, families, careers. One of them, Mari, gave me a lift home the other night. Outwardly she has everything going for her, but her job as a child therapist was getting her down.

'I was ready to throw myself in the Bay the other night,' she said cheerfully. Thank God for Bridge. Sometimes I wonder how I could carry on without it.'

Whenever I hear words like that – and I do hear them quite often – I think of course of Greta. I'm glad and grateful that I can pay it forward, this love of Bridge she passed on to me. I still see her as the cantankerous old autocrat, but also the young maid, making her way. I give thanks for her life, what she gave to me, am proud to have known her and ashamed to have doubted her. I think back sometimes to that maid in Greta's elevator, telling me she was blessed. I don't think Greta felt herself to be particularly blessed, and maybe she wasn't. But now I know I have been.

And I'm sure too that she had her time and place and role in the world, as we all seek.

Printed in Great Britain
by Amazon

67787382R00130